THE SECRETS OF MAGIC
ELEMENTALS ACADEMY
BOOK TWO

MICHELLE MADOW

DREAMSCAPE PUBLISHING

THE SECRETS OF MAGIC
Elementals Academy 2

Published by Dreamscape Publishing

Copyright © 2022 Michelle Madow

ISBN: 9798840902806

This book is a work of fiction. Though some actual towns, cities, and locations may be mentioned, they are used in a fictitious manner and the events and occurrences were invented in the mind and imagination of the author. Any similarities of characters or names used within to any person past, present, or future is coincidental.

All rights reserved. No part of this book may be used or reproduced in any manner whatsoever without written permission from the author. Brief quotations may be embodied in critical articles or reviews.

CHAPTER ONE

"Two days ago, Elementals Academy was infiltrated by twelve nymphs whose minds had been poisoned by magic."

Kate stood in front of the lake, the pink-orange rays of sunset shimmering over her skin. Nicole stood on one side of her, and Blake on the other. Two teachers stood with them as well. Mason, the head teacher of the air elementals, along with the head teacher of the water elementals—a woman named Mira.

Behind them was a table with eight urns on it.

I wrapped my arms around myself and shivered. It was freezing outside—so cold that the lake had frozen over. The bonfire in front of the lake created a bubble of heat large enough to warm all the students and teachers gathered in black for the ceremony, but the cold still crawled beneath my skin and into my bones.

I stood next to Jamie, the two of us amongst the other air elementals.

Alyssa wasn't with us.

The parents of the fallen students stood in the front row.

They weren't nymphs, I thought as I listened to Kate speak.

Because the women who had attacked the school were goddesses. They were the twelve handmaidens of the Norse goddess Freya. But Kate couldn't say that. Because only Kate, Nicole, Blake, Zane, and I knew about the return of the gods and monsters from Norse mythology.

Telling anyone else about it would cause chaos. So, Kate had created this lie, and it seemed like everyone was buying it.

Of course they were buying it. Why would they doubt their trusted headmistress?

"Thanks to your training, quick action, and ability to work together in a fight, we were able to kill all twelve nymphs," Kate continued.

Another lie.

Well, a half lie.

Because they were certainly *able* to kill all twelve handmaidens. But they hadn't.

They'd kept one for questioning and had locked her in a secure location somewhere on campus.

As a student, I wasn't privy to where that location

was. I was also pretty sure that "questioning" was a nice way of saying they were putting her through multiple torture sessions.

Torture sessions that might wear her down to the point where she told them the truth about Zane.

I refused to look over to the left, where the water students were gathered. Because every time I saw Zane, I was reminded about what he was.

An immortal.

A supernatural from Norse mythology, sent here by his people to spy on the school. I highly suspected that his "close family friend" Vera was an immortal as well.

It had been a few days since the attack, and he'd texted me on each one of them—multiple times a day. But I hadn't replied. I didn't know what to say.

"And now, we lay the eight of them to rest in the place where they feel most at home," Kate finished up her speech. "In their element."

Everyone was silent. The only sound was the rustling of wind blowing through the bare branches of the trees in the forest.

"We'll start by honoring the two students of my element—earth—by burying their ashes in the roots of the trees." Kate removed one of the urns from the table, and Nicole took the other. "Daisy Collins and Sage LaPorte."

She and Nicole walked to the edge of the forest, where two small holes had already been dug. Kate poured the ashes from the urn she was holding into the first hole, and Nicole handed the second urn to her so she could pour its ashes into the other.

Despite knowing otherwise, none of this felt real to me. It was like I was watching a movie instead of living it in real life.

Once the urns were emptied, Kate kneeled and pressed her hands into the dirt. She muttered a prayer—so quietly that I couldn't make out the words—and energy buzzed through the ground beneath my feet.

She got up, stepped back, and revealed two trees in the places where the girls' ashes had been buried. I didn't know the girls, but my heart swelled with grief for the lives lost.

Next up was fire. One student and one teacher from their element had lost their lives in the attack.

Kate announced their names. Then Blake took the first urn, and Nicole took the second. He walked to the bonfire and poured the ashes into the flames. As he did, the top of the fire danced higher, tendrils of smoke winding around each other and floating up into the sky. The warm scent of campfire filled the brisk air, and when I inhaled, it was sharp inside my lungs.

Jamie reached for my hand and squeezed it. When I glanced over at her, I saw small tears making their way down her cheeks.

Many others were sniffling and rubbing tears out of their eyes, too.

I held back any tears that attempted to leak through. I'd never been much of a crier—especially in public. I saved it all up for when I was by myself.

Unlike me, Jamie wasn't one to bottle her emotions. If Alyssa were here with us, I knew she'd be the same.

I swallowed down more tears at the thought of the quiet room in my suite where my bouncy, lively friend had once lived.

Water had the fewest casualties, with only one amongst the fallen. Their head teacher—Mira—removed the urn from the table, spun around, and walked toward the lake. She took a few steps along its frozen surface, kneeled onto the ice, and placed the urn by her side. She held both hands in front of her, and the ice under her palms melted, leaving a circular hole leading into the water. It looked like what people in the movies did when they went ice fishing.

As Mira poured the ashes into the hole, I shuddered at the thought of being laid to rest in such a cold, dark place.

Once finished, she held her palms over the hole again to freeze it. The newly formed ice was slicker and shinier than that around it.

She didn't cry. Water elementals weren't known for being outwardly emotional.

Part of me wanted to glance at Zane to try to see what

he was feeling. He knew the handmaidens. Did he feel responsible for the attack on the school? Were these deaths partly on his hands?

I gave in and tried to glance as subtly as possible.

A second after I did, his gaze locked on mine.

His ice-blue eyes were sharp and cold, like he was angry at me for freezing him out. The rest of his perfectly sculpted features gave away no emotions. He was otherworldly and dangerous, and now that I knew he was an immortal and not a witch, I didn't know how I'd missed it before. There was something eerily *inhuman* about him. Not like witches were technically humans, but we were far closer to them than he was.

I sucked in another sharp breath that stung my lungs, and then forced myself to look ahead, where Mason was picking up the first of the three urns that contained the ashes of the air elementals. Kate picked up the second, and Nicole the third.

"Melissa Foster," Kate said the name of the first air elemental who'd fallen. "Parker Palmer. And Doreen Clarke."

I'd eaten lunch with Parker and Doreen on my first day at Elementals Academy. They were Alyssa's friends.

Alyssa, Parker, and Doreen had been leaving the dining hall together when the handmaidens attacked. They'd been taken down in the courtyard, and they'd fought as hard as they could until Mason helped them kill the handmaiden off.

Doreen and Parker hadn't made it.

Alyssa had barely escaped with her life.

Visiting her in the infirmity had been one of the hardest things I'd ever done. She was in a coma, on life support, with what the doctor had informed me was severe brain trauma. I would have thought she was peacefully sleeping, if not for the dark, purple bruises staining her face.

And because the injury had been caused by a being from Norse mythology, Nicole's healing magic couldn't help her.

I'd prayed to Hecate last night, pleading with her to do something to fix this. I did so again right now, as Mason used his magic to make the wind pick up around him.

Hecate was the goddess Alyssa had turned to more than any other in the Greek pantheon.

Unlike the other elements, Mason didn't pour the ashes out of the urn. He used his magic to float them up into the wind, which funneled them up to the sky like a small tornado. The ashes disappeared into the clouds until all three urns were empty.

A woman sobbed loudly in the front row. Likely the mother of one of the fallen students.

My heart broke for her.

If Zane hadn't been there with me to kill the handmaiden who'd attacked us, it could have been my mother up there, grieving for me. Although that would have involved her learning about witches and coming to the academy. It would have been a lot for her to handle all at once. I imagined she would have ended up in some sort of massive shock.

I needed to tell my mom the truth eventually, especially given how intuitive she was. One way or the other, she'd pick up on the fact that something was off. And I wanted to be the one who told her everything.

Once things at the academy fell into a routine again, I'd ask Kate about the best way to go about telling her. Because if something ever happened to me, I wanted my mom to be prepared. I couldn't keep the truth of my life—of who I am—secret from her forever.

"We wish the fallen students safe passage with Charon to the Underworld," Kate continued once the final empty urn had been placed back onto the table. "And, as they died as heroes protecting the school, we can rest assured knowing they'll have a peaceful afterlife in Elysium. So we won't say goodbye forever. Instead, we say *is to epanidín*. The Greek phrase for 'until we meet again.'"

CHAPTER TWO

The parents of the fallen students remained at the lake after the ceremony to bid farewell to their children in private.

The rest of us returned to our dorms, where we ate dinner.

Air students were notoriously loud—they were the partiers of the school. But the loss of their friends hung heavy in the air, and tonight, we ate in near silence. Darkness had descended upon the normally bright common area, so strong that it blanketed my skin.

After dinner, Jamie followed me to my room. She'd been spending a lot of time in here these past two days. I wasn't sure if it was because *she* didn't want to be alone, or if she didn't want *me* to be alone, given how eerie it was for Alyssa's room to be so quiet.

I suspected it was a bit of both. Most air students were super extraverted and hated being alone.

I was the exception.

Because I wasn't an air elemental.

My affinity was for metal and gems. Kate suspected it meant I was a descendent of Hades, although I still hadn't been claimed by my godly ancestor, so we didn't know for sure.

Given that Hades was the god of the Underworld, and a loner according to the textbooks, it could explain my introverted tendencies. Like how I wanted Jamie to leave so I could curl up with a book and try to forget reality for a few hours.

But Jamie had been one of Alyssa's best friends.

She *was* one of Alyssa's best friends. Alyssa was still alive—I shouldn't think about her in past tense. Either way, I didn't have the heart to ask Jamie to give me space right away. I'd indulge her for a little while. It was the right thing to do.

She plopped onto my bed, making herself at home. "Do you have anything to drink?" she asked.

"I have Coke," I said. "Regular—not diet."

I hated diet drinks. They tasted like chemicals.

"That's not what I meant," she said. "I need a *real* drink."

I glanced at the door to my bathroom, which connected my room to Alyssa's. Her mini fridge was always stocked with wine.

Jamie's eyes followed mine. "She'd want us to have it," she finally said. "She wouldn't want it to sit there useless, not being enjoyed." She nodded, as if confirming her own statement.

I froze and pointed my thumb toward the door. "Do you want me…?" I started, unable to finish the question.

"No—you stay here. I'll get it." She jumped out of the bed and made her way to the door.

I was sure Jamie had her own alcohol in her minifridge, but suspected it was simply an excuse for her to take a personal moment in her best friend's room.

With Jamie now preoccupied, I grabbed my pajamas and hurried into the bathroom to change. After I finished, my gaze went to the mirror. My skin was paler than normal, and my jet-black hair was greasy at the top, like it hadn't been washed in days.

Which, to be fair, it hadn't.

But my days-old hair wasn't why I was staring. It was because when I looked into my green eyes, a buzz traveled over my skin. Like someone was on the other side looking back at me.

Someone's there.

I'd been feeling that way around mirrors a lot lately. It was why I'd taken an extra sheet and flung it over the full-length mirror in my room.

I narrowed my eyes at my reflection, as if I could scare

whatever was looking back at me away. It didn't work. So, not wanting to look in the mirror for any longer, I went back to my room.

Jamie was already there with an open bottle of wine and two full Solo cups in front of her.

"Here." She handed one of the cups to me. "I think we both need this right now."

I'd never been the sort of person to say I *needed* a drink.

I also didn't like to watch my friends drink alone.

So I sat down on the floor next to her and took the cup.

"To…" She paused and held up her cup, like she was trying to find something to cheers to.

"To nothing," I said simply. "Let's just drink."

We didn't bother clinking our glasses together. Instead, she gave me a single nod, and we each took a sip.

The wine was good. I'd expect nothing else from Alyssa's stash.

"So," she said after a few moments of silence. "Zane was staring at you for the entire ceremony."

I froze at the sound of his name, the cup of wine halfway to my lips.

"He wasn't," I said, even though I could feel in my bones that it was true. I'd *felt* his gaze on me just as strongly as I could feel whoever was watching me through the mirror.

"He definitely was," she said.

Irritation coursed through me, and I took a long sip of my wine, as if it could dull my emotions. Because the last thing I should have been thinking about during the ceremony was Zane, and the way his eyes had glowed when we'd kissed.

My soulmate.

No, I thought, as if pushing the thought of him from my mind could push the connection between us from existence.

"I don't care about him," I said. "He's an asshole."

"He's into you."

"Why are we even talking about this?" I snapped. Jamie flinched back, and I took a deep breath to calm myself before continuing. "I just mean that students were just killed. They're *dead.* Alyssa is in the infirmary fighting for her life. The last thing we should be doing is gossiping about guys."

Jamie stared sullenly into her cup, unable to meet my eyes. "Sorry," she mumbled, and when she looked back up at me, her soulful eyes were glassy with tears. "Of course I care. It's just that I feel…" She paused, figuring out how to express her emotion. "Helpless."

"Because you couldn't save Alyssa."

"I tried. But she just… froze up."

Jamie had been with Alyssa and the others when the handmaiden had attacked them.

She'd seen Doreen and Parker die.

"You're not helpless," I told her. "Mason said that if it wasn't for you, Alyssa would probably be dead right now."

"Instead she's withering away in there, stuck between life and death," she said. "She might never wake up. I'd prefer going to Elysium than being stuck like *that.*"

"Don't say that," I said. "Nicole will figure out how to heal her."

"Yeah." She shrugged. "Maybe."

Not knowing what to say, I took another sip of wine. Because I was one of the few people at the school who knew the truth about why Nicole couldn't heal Alyssa, or anyone else who had sustained injuries in the attack.

Her magic didn't work on injuries made by the Norse. But I couldn't say that, since Jamie had no idea that the Norse gods were real.

I had to act clueless, and I hated every second of it.

"It's not that I don't care," Jamie continued. "I obviously care. I was just trying to distract myself."

"Oh." I frowned, although I supposed it made sense that Jamie would distract herself with the one thing that always seemed to be on her mind—guys. "How's it going with Greg?"

The least I could do for her was play along.

"It's not." She smiled slyly. "I'm back with Topher."

"Cool." I nodded, since as much as Jamie's eyes tended to wander, it seemed like she *always* ended up back with Topher—the quiet earth elemental I hadn't even met yet. "Are things going well with him?"

"They are," she said with a slight smile. "He's spending more time with me than he used to. It's like ever since the attack, he appreciates me more. Because I didn't end up like..." She trailed off and glanced at the door to Alyssa's room, her eyes darkening again.

"He's glad you're okay," I said.

"He is." She took a large sip of wine—more than half of her glass was empty now. She paused for a bit, looking blankly into space, then said, "It seems like all conversation now comes back to the attack."

"Yeah," I agreed. "But that'll change in time."

Maybe.

Because it didn't feel like the threat of the Norse gods was going away anytime soon. The opposite, actually. Because this was only their first attack. There was so much going on behind the scenes that I didn't know about.

There was only one person around here who did.

Zane.

And maybe Vera.

I couldn't avoid talking to him for much longer. Especially because he was the one person I knew who might have an answer about how to help Alyssa.

Jamie finished the rest of her wine in one long, final

swig. "I think I'm gonna head out," she said. "Thanks for chatting."

"Are you sure?" I asked, even though relief filled me at the thought of finally getting to be alone.

"I'm gonna head to Topher's." She reached for the bottle of wine, but stopped halfway there. "Is it okay if I take this?"

"Go wild."

"Cool." She smiled. "Thanks."

"No problem," I said. "Have fun."

She smirked and waggled her eyebrows. "Trust me—I will."

We stood up, and she glanced around my room, worried.

"Are you sure you're okay here alone?" she asked.

"Why wouldn't I be okay?"

"It's just so... *quiet.*"

"I like the quiet," I said.

"Right," she said, as if she'd forgotten. Which she might have, since literally no one else in the air dorm had an introverted bone in their body. "You should hang out with me and Topher soon. I think you'd get along."

"Cool," I said. "That'll be great."

It truly would. From what I'd seen of them so far, I liked the earth elementals. They were bookish. Introverted. Much more my speed.

Jamie and I finished saying goodbye, and then I was

finally alone. I had homework to do, but it wasn't due for two days. And while I normally wasn't a procrastinator, all I wanted right now was to make some hot chocolate, curl up under the covers, and read.

So that was exactly what I did.

Unfortunately, my mind drifted after a few pages. To the one thing it hadn't stopped drifting to since I'd arrived at the academy—Zane.

I cursed inwardly. Why wouldn't he get out of my damn head?

Annoyed at myself, I placed the book down on my stomach, reached for my phone, and pulled up my text message chain with Zane.

It was full of unanswered messages from him that had been piling up over the past few days.

Hope you're doing okay.

I heard about Alyssa. I'm so sorry.

Can we talk?

I need to see to you. We need to talk about what happened.

I stared at the blinking curser and hovered my thumbs above the keys. But they stayed there, not touching the screen. Because I had no idea what to say to him. Part of me hated him and wanted to scream at him for not doing anything to stop the attack. Part of me wanted to sit down with him and hear him out. And another part—the part I hated the most—wanted to kiss him again.

I didn't trust myself around him. Mainly because

whenever I was around him, every bone in my body told me to trust him, and I should know better than that. He'd been keeping his true identity secret from everyone in this school since he'd started here over two years ago. He was an expert liar. I had no reason to trust him—especially since he'd lied to me, too.

I also owed him my life.

I was still staring at the blinking curser when my phone buzzed, and my heart leaped. But the text that appeared at the top wasn't from Zane. It was from Nicole.

Disappointment and relief coursed through me at the same time.

Want to come to dinner at the cottage tomorrow night?

"The cottage" was Kinsley Cottage—the house on campus where Nicole, Blake, and Kate lived.

I pulled up my texts with Nicole and stared at the invite.

Why was she inviting me to dinner at the cottage? As far as I knew, no other students were asked to dine with the original Elementals as a simple social call.

Did they know about Zane?

A ball of anxiety formed in my throat, and I tried to swallow it down. Because I was pretty sure that Blake had been suspicious of the story Zane had told him back in the forest.

Maybe he'd told the others that he was suspicious of Zane, and they'd looked into it and figured out the truth?

Maybe they knew I was keeping his secret for him, and they were inviting me to dinner to try to force the answers out of me?

I tapped back to my text chain with Zane. Maybe I should ask if *he* was okay?

But if Blake and the others had taken him in for questioning, there was no way he'd have his phone on him.

I could also text him to let him know that Nicole had invited me for dinner at the cottage. I had a feeling he'd want to know.

And then what? Make him paranoid that I might turn on him? Reassure him that his secret was safe with me?

Was his secret safe with me?

I didn't know. Because I was a terrible liar. If Nicole and the others confronted me about Zane, I doubted I'd be able to keep the truth from them. I didn't *want* to keep the truth from them. I was just doing it because of this strange loyalty to Zane that I couldn't shake, no matter how hard I tried.

I hated this. Especially because there was no one I could talk to about it.

You can talk to Zane, an annoying voice said in the back of my mind.

I pushed it away. Because Nicole was waiting for an answer, and the longer I delayed responding, the more suspicious it might seem.

Sure, I replied. *What time?*

7:00. See you then!

I sent the thumbs up reaction, then closed out the texts and placed my phone face-down on my nightstand, refusing to look at the texts from Zane again.

CHAPTER THREE

Dinner at Kinsley Cottage was welcomely relaxed. The four of us sat around the kitchen table, each eating a piece of steak that had been cooked by Blake. It felt like a normal family dinner—the type I had with Lara back home when I went over to her house to eat with her and her parents.

As I cut into my steak and took a bite—medium-rare, just how I liked it—my thoughts went to Zane.

Again.

Because he basically only ate meat. He'd forced down some cheese for me at our picnic in the woods, but it was clear he'd found it unenjoyable.

I assumed it had to do with his being an immortal. They must only eat meat, or something of the sort. It was on my mental list of the many questions I had for him.

I could have tried looking up information on what he

was—the technical term for it was *immortal giant*—but I hadn't yet. I didn't want to wonder what was true and what wasn't. I wanted to hear the answers from Zane.

Nicole, Kate, and Blake watched me as I ate, and I fidgeted uneasily. So far, the main thing we'd talked about was the attack and the ceremony last night.

The entire time, I felt like I was being watched. Partly by the mirror hanging on the wall, and partly by Blake.

Other than that, there were no hints that they were suspicious of anything. Which left one big question.

"Why am I here?" I asked Kate. I tightened my grip around my utensils, preparing for anything.

The metal fork and knife buzzed in my grip, like they were letting me know they were there for me.

"I'm going to guess you haven't received a token from Hades since the last time we were here?" Kate responded to my question with one of her own.

"Or from any of the gods," Nicole chimed in. "Since we don't officially know you're a descendent of Hades."

I relaxed instantly.

Because *of course* that was why I was there. They wanted to chat about the secret I was keeping with them —Kate's theory that I was a descendent of Hades, since I had elemental control over metal and gems. Not the secret I was keeping with Zane.

If they knew anything about Zane, I doubted they would have been so polite about it.

"I haven't," I said. "But trust me—when I do, you'll be the first ones I tell."

"I figured as much, but I don't want to keep waiting around," Kate said. "I invited you here because I want to take action to confirm that my theory about you being a descendent of Hades is correct. Normally I wouldn't support forcing something like this, but your magic is unique, and we have a conflict with the Norse gods to handle. So I think it's best that we know exactly what type of magic you're dealing with here."

"It sounds like you want to use me as a weapon." I shivered at the thought. Because weapons were used for one big thing—war.

Did she think we were going to go to war with the Norse gods?

"We're all weapons," Nicole said. "It's why we get to train here for free. And like it or not, you're one of us now."

I paused and sipped my water. Because crazily enough, I sort of did like it. As daunting as everything they were telling me was, I finally felt like I'd found a place where I belonged. A home. And if understanding more about my magic could help keep this place intact, then I was all for it.

"I want to learn about my ancestry, too," I finally said. "But I thought we didn't find out who we were descended from until they leave us a token."

"We don't," Kate said. "But there's a first time for everything."

We shared a smile, since it was the same thing she'd told me after I'd failed my elemental placement test.

"All right." I straightened, feeling inexplicably ready for this. "How do we 'take action?' Because I feel like you can't just give Hades a call in the Underworld. Unless you can?"

"That would be too easy, wouldn't it?" Kate said with another kind smile. "But we can do something sort of similar."

"Like what?"

"We can write him a letter."

I almost laughed, because that certainly hadn't been the response I'd expected. "You can address a letter to the Underworld?"

"Again—not that easy," Kate said. "But we can try to get in contact with Hermes—the messenger god. He's one of the few gods who can go back and forth to the Underworld."

"And he'll do that for you? Just because you ask?" I glanced at Nicole and Blake, as if they could give me a second opinion.

"Doubtful," Blake said, and from the knowing look he gave Kate, I had a feeling he wasn't totally on board with this plan. "The gods never do anything without asking for something in return."

"Sort of like the fae," I said.

"The what?" Nicole blinked a few times, confused.

"The fae," I repeated. "Faeries."

Her expression remained blank.

"I guess they don't actually exist here," I said.

"I knew what you were talking about," Kate said. "I also love to read. And you're correct—as far as we know, fae don't exist. But we also didn't think the Norse gods existed until now. And the fae are part of Celtic folklore, so if the Norse gods exist somewhere, then maybe the fae do, too."

"You guys can talk about this later," Nicole broke in—I had a feeling she didn't read as much as Kate and I did. "How do you feel about the idea of writing this letter?"

"You're all on board?" I specifically looked at Blake when I asked.

"For writing the letter—yes," he said stiffly. "Then we'll hear what Hermes asks from us and make a decision from there."

"Sounds reasonable," I said. "But what about Hades? Is *he* reasonable? Will he be cool with getting a letter asking him to verify the fact that he's my ancestor? Because from what I've learned about the gods so far, they can be a little..." I paused, not wanting to use a word that offended them, especially since one of the gods was Nicole's father.

"Volatile?" Kate supplied.

"Exactly." I breathed out in relief, since she agreed.

"Blake and I have actually been to the Underworld and have met Hades," Nicole said. "We had a rather enjoyable time there." She glanced at Blake, and I could have *sworn* he blushed. "Compared to most of the gods, Hades is very level-headed. And his wife Persephone helps keep him as open-minded as she can."

"And you think she'd be open-minded to the fact that he had a child outside their marriage?" I asked sarcastically, since I hardly saw *that* conversation going well.

Although given the number of descendants most of the gods had, I figured it wasn't an uncommon one to have.

"I'm going ask Hermes to tell Hades to open the letter in private," Kate said. "Hades can decide what to do from there."

"*If* Hermes delivers the letter at all," Blake added.

"I'm trying to be positive here," Kate said, and she refocused on me. "But at the end of the day, this is up to you. So, what do you say? Are you open to trying this?"

"Sure," I said, since I couldn't think of anything I had to lose. "But it's not every day that I write a letter to a god who may or may not be one of my long-lost ancestors. Do you think you can help me figure out what to say?"

"I was planning on it," she said. "I've already written up a few ideas of where we can start. So, after we're done with dinner, I'll get my laptop, and we can begin."

As we finished eating, Blake and Nicole told me all about their journey to the Underworld. It was wild, and there was a good reason why Blake had blushed—apparently there are places in the Underworld that can be very romantic, especially for two teens in love who thought they might be facing their final few days together.

Once we finished, I helped Nicole and Blake bring the dishes to the sink, and Kate went upstairs to get her laptop.

I joined Kate when she returned, and Nicole and Blake continued cleaning up. She set the laptop down in front of us on the table and brought up a Word document. She hadn't just jotted down a few ideas—she'd created a detailed outline of the points we needed to make.

"We'll write the letter on the computer and edit it until it's ready," she said. "After that, you'll write it out by hand. It'll be more personal that way."

"Sure." I already felt overwhelmed just by looking at what Kate had written down. There were so many bullet points of information that my head was spinning thinking about how to turn this into an actual letter.

"How about you try first?" Kate opened a fresh document and faced the laptop toward me. "Write out whatever you're feeling. I can help you from there."

I stared at the blinking curser and hovered my fingers above the keys.

Dear Hades, I started.

No. That didn't feel right.

I deleted the "dear," so it would just start with his name. Best not to act overly familiar too quickly.

Hi! My name's Summer Donovan. I have magic over metal. Do you think I might be descended from you?

Casual. To the point.

Way too perky.

By Kate's frown, I could tell she agreed.

"Maybe pretend like you're writing to a professor?" she suggested. "Or writing an essay for school?"

I highlighted what I'd written and clicked delete. In less than a second, the words vanished from the page.

Before I could take another stab at it, someone knocked on the front door.

Kate jumped and looked into the living room. Nicole and Blake stopped doing the dishes, looking equally as confused.

"I take it you don't get many visitors?" I asked.

"No one comes to the cottage uninvited." Kate shut the laptop, stood, and headed into the other room. Blake and Nicole followed, and I walked with them into the living room as well.

Kate was standing next to the window, poking her head through the drapes and angling her neck to try to peer onto the porch.

"Who is it?" Nicole asked.

"It's a woman." Kate turned back around to face us.

"But she's wearing a hood, so I can't make out her features."

I glanced at the others, uneasy.

"I'll get my arrows." Nicole zipped out into the hall and up the stairs.

"I thought the school's boundary had been strengthened after the attack," Blake said to Kate. "None of the Norse should be able to get through."

"The Elders saw to it," she said. "Whoever this woman is, she must have been inside the school's boundaries before they were created."

Nicole returned with her bow in one hand and a pack of arrows at her back.

"I don't think we're at risk of harm," Kate said, and she looked to me. "But maybe you should stand behind Nicole, just in case."

She saw me as weak. I hated it.

Then again, I *was* weak compared to them. And I lacked the years of experience that they had.

As I walked to stand behind Nicole, I eyed the room for possible ways to protect myself. There was a fireplace, and next to it was a poker, a shovel, and a sweep. All of them were made of metal. I reached out with my mind and *felt* them sitting there.

If needed, I could call one to me. Definitely the poker, since it looked like it could do the most damage of the three.

"Lower your weapon," Kate said to Nicole. "Whoever this is, we don't want to put them on defense from the get-go."

"Fine." Nicole rolled her eyes and reluctantly lowered her bow.

Blake's hands glowed orange with the threat of fire.

"All right." Kate smoothed her hair, took a deep breath, and opened the door.

A woman wearing a long black cloak stood on the porch, the hood draping so low over her face that it was impossible to make out her features. It was like she was dressed as the grim reaper.

My heart pounded faster, and my palms felt clammy. Did she have a connection with Hades? Had she come here for me?

Before I could think about it anymore, she stepped forward, reached up, and pushed the hood off her face.

I sucked in a sharp breath, surprise and confusion rushing through my body.

"Hecate?" Kate said, at the same time as I said, "Mom?"

CHAPTER FOUR

I stepped around Nicole and stared at my mom, shocked.

She looked *different*.

Her long hair, as black as my own, was shinier than I remembered. Her dark blue eyes glowed a supernatural violet in the moonlight, and her snow-white skin had an otherworldly glow to it that reminded me of Kate's.

For the first time ever, my soft-spoken mom looked intimidating.

Hecate, I repeated what Kate had said in my mind.

No way. She had to be wrong. Because that didn't make any sense.

My mom's strangely purple eyes were focused on me.

"What are you doing here?" I finally asked.

Kate looked back and forth between us, appearing as shocked as I felt. "You two know each other?"

"That's my mom," I said. "She's not…"

I couldn't say the name out loud. *Hecate.* It was so incredibly ridiculous.

At the same time, the slight changes in my mom's appearance said otherwise.

"May I come in?" my mom asked Kate, completely ignoring my question.

"Of course." Kate stepped to the side to let her pass. She was so focused on my mom that she didn't look at me.

Once inside, my mom closed the door behind her, studied me, and gave me a small smile. "You look strong," she said. "Magic suits you."

Part of me wanted to run to her and give her a huge hug.

The other part was betrayed. Hurt. *Angry.*

I reached out with my mind to the tools next to the fireplace, and one of them flew into my palm.

The broom.

Because as confused as I felt, I didn't actually want to hurt my mom.

"Such strong control of your powers already," she said. "As would be expected, given the magic surrounding you as you grew up."

Nicole stepped up to stand next to me, still holding the bow. "You're Summer's mom," she said. "But you're also Hecate."

"Correct," my mom said, and my eyes widened at the confirmation.

"That means Summer's a demigod?" Nicole asked.

"I'm adopted," I said quickly. "I'm not a demigod."

My mom pressed her lips together and hesitated. "I'm afraid I haven't been completely honest with you," she said, and the floor bottomed out beneath my feet as I waited for her to continue. "It's true that I'm not your birth mother. But Kate was correct in her theory about your elemental magic. Because you *are* related to Hades. You're his daughter."

"I knew it," Kate said with a knowing smirk.

"Wait," I asked my mom. "I'm a demigod? And you've known this whole time?"

The word felt foreign when I spoke it.

A *demigod.*

If it was true, then my father was Hades. *The* Hades that ruled the Underworld. A god. And one of the scarier, more mysterious gods at that.

My entire world shifted on its axis.

"It explains why you got the hang of using your magic so quickly," Kate said excitedly. "Demigods are stronger than regular witches, and they have an easier time learning how to access and control their magic."

"Okay," I said slowly, barely aware of the fact that I was speaking. "Got it."

"Are you okay?" my mom asked in concern.

No, not my mom.

Hecate.

The goddess of witchcraft. I'd been raised by the goddess of witchcraft.

"I'm... processing." It was the only word that could explain what was going on in my mind.

No one spoke.

Then a ton of emotions slammed into me at once, and I glared at my mom, angry tears forming in my eyes. "You lied to me," I said simply. "For my entire life."

"I did what I had to do to protect you."

"To protect me from what?"

"From your father." Her eyes that were familiar but not filled with intensity.

"Why would I have to be protected from Hades?" I couldn't call this strange man my *dad*, or *father*, or whatever he was supposed to be to me.

"Because I've known Hades for a long, long time," she said. "Longer than you could possibly comprehend. And he doesn't believe his family belongs in the world of the living. If he knew you existed, he'd do everything in his power to drag you down to the Underworld."

"Back up," I said. "He doesn't know I *exist?*"

"He didn't know your mom was pregnant with you," she said. "She delivered you secretly and entrusted you with me for your protection. She wanted you to live a normal life, so she gave me explicit instructions to hide you—and your magic. So I bound your powers. Although that spell unraveled on the night of the Northern Lights."

"You know what happened that night?" Kate interrupted.

"I don't," she said. "At least, not specifically. But I think it's safe to assume it had something to do with the Norse gods."

Blake studied me suspiciously, then turned to my mom. "So you're saying Summer's magic could be related to the Norse gods?"

I froze.

Because my magic *was* connected to the Norse.

To Zane.

Of course, that was assuming Zane had told the truth that whatever had happened between us in the forest was a soulmate bond. But if he was telling the truth—and I did think he was—then my soul was connected to his. And likely to his magic as well.

"Not at all," my mom said calmly. "Summer's biological mother didn't have a drop of Norse blood in her body."

Blake nodded, although he didn't look satisfied with that answer.

"What do you know about my birth mother?" I asked. "Who is she? And how did you know her?"

"I'm afraid that's all I'm able to say on that matter," she said, and from her tone, I knew she wasn't going to budge. "But I believe you're meant to help us defend ourselves against the Norse gods. As the only daughter of Hades, you could be a powerful asset to our side."

"You think there's going to be a war."

"I think we need to hope for the best, but plan for the worst."

"Right." I'd heard that phrase before—it was the same one newscasters used when preparing Floridians for hurricanes.

And if she wanted to believe that my magic emerged to help the Greeks against the Norse, then I'd let her run with that theory. Because as long as she and the others believed that, then they couldn't trace this back to Zane.

If it had to do with Zane.

"You really think Hades would force me into the Underworld if he knew about me?" I asked the first question that popped into my mind to change the subject.

"I do," she said. "It's why I had to come here to tell you the truth now—before you sent that letter."

"How did you know we were writing the letter?" I glanced at the mirror on the bookshelf, and that familiar prickle of being watched crawled up my arms and down my spine.

"I have my ways," she said.

"Like spying on people through mirrors?"

She flinched, and worry flashed across her face for a split-second. "I can't spy on anyone through mirrors," she said, even though I knew she wasn't the one watching us right now, since she was in the room with us.

So who was it?

Kate cursed, and I did a double-take—she didn't seem like the type to use bad language. Nicole and Blake looked surprised, too. "I forgot about the mirrors," Kate said. "You mentioned them after the attack, but things got so crazy after that..." She trailed off, then walked over to the mirror and placed it face-down on the shelf.

The prickly feeling of being watched disappeared.

"Like I was saying, the truth of your identity can't leave this room," my mom continued. "The more people who know, the more likely it is that Hades will find out. So the four of you must keep this a secret. Understood?"

We all said various versions of yes.

As if I needed another secret to keep right now. It almost felt like I had no choice, but of course I had a choice.

I was choosing to protect myself.

Just like I was choosing to protect Zane.

"I have one more question," I said, and my mom looked to me to continue. "After I came to Elementals Academy, the Elders talked to you to make you believe another story about why I left Hollins for a school in Virginia. Nicole told me." I glanced at Nicole, and she nodded in confirmation. Then I turned back to my mom.

"You even acted clueless on the phone. But how did the Elders not know that you have magic?"

"I'm the goddess of witchcraft." She smiled knowingly. "If I don't want someone to know I have magic, then they won't know."

"Got it," I said, since along with not being able to comprehend how long my mom had lived, I had a feeling that the amount of magic she had was beyond what I could possibly imagine.

"I have a question, too," Nicole said, and my mom looked to her to continue. "Why can't my magic heal injuries made by the Norse?"

"I'm afraid I don't know the answer to that." She frowned. "It's not in any of the ancient texts."

"Do you have any other way of finding the answer?" I asked. "Because my best friend here was hurt during the attack on the school. Badly. We need to figure out how to heal her."

"Careful," my mom chided. "Lara wouldn't appreciate you calling someone else your best friend."

For the first time since walking into the cottage, she sounded like my mom and not Hecate.

"It's different," I said.

"I know. I'll ask around, although I can't guarantee that anyone will have the answer."

"Thanks."

"Yeah," Nicole agreed. "I feel kind of useless without my magic."

"You're not useless," Blake said. "No one can shoot a bow and arrow better than you."

She shrugged, looking troubled despite his compliment.

"I'll start asking around," my mom said. "In the meantime, I need you to stay under the radar. Can you do that?"

"Staying under the radar hasn't exactly been my specialty recently," I said.

"Then I need you to *make* it your specialty." The laser-focused expression in her eyes made it clear that this wasn't up for discussion.

"Sure." I shuffled on my feet, uneasy. "I'll do my best."

"Good," she said, and then she spun around, walked out the front door, and vanished into the night.

CHAPTER FIVE

We looked after her in silence.

"Wow," Nicole spoke first. "Hecate is your mom."

"My adopted mom," I corrected her, taking a moment to organize my thoughts. "I was raised by the goddess of witchcraft."

"It's pretty insane," she said.

"I guess it explains all the tarot cards and candle burning and chakra stuff."

"I thought you said your mom had no connection with magic?" Kate asked.

"She had no connection with *elemental* magic," I said. "But tons of normal people are into all that new age stuff. How was I supposed to know she could do it for real?"

"You weren't," Nicole said. "My mom's into some of that stuff, too, and she's definitely *not* a witch."

I relaxed a bit, grateful for the validation.

"Now that we know my theory is correct, there's more stuff we need to talk about," Kate said, snapping back to business. "We should sit. Maybe with an after-dinner drink?"

"What did you have in mind?" I asked, taken by surprise. We hadn't had any alcohol at dinner, and Kate didn't strike me as someone who was into drinking.

"I can make a pretty good old fashioned, if I do say so myself," she said with pride. "How many will it be?"

We all said we wanted one, and Kate headed to the kitchen.

"She's good at mixing things up," Nicole said, apparently noticing my surprise. "You'll see."

About ten minutes later, we were all sitting in the living room, drinks in hand. I'd never had an old fashioned before, but as promised, it was delicious.

"Another thing I wanted to bring up with you tonight was your living situation," Kate said once we were settled in. "Since you're not an air elemental, I was thinking you might want to move into the cottage with us. But after what Hecate said about staying under the radar, I changed my mind. I think you should stay where you are."

"Wow." My heart warmed at the offer—well, at the offer she *would* have made. This cottage felt much more like a potential home than the air dorm, since I wasn't similar to the air elementals in the slightest. "For what it's worth, I would have taken you up on it."

"Maybe someday," she said hopefully. "But given what we just learned, I think it's more important than ever that you blend in. Which means pretending to be an air elemental."

"You want me to hide my real magic." The words felt hollow as I spoke them.

Would the secrets ever stop piling up?

There were so many of them that it was starting to feel hard to breathe—like the secrets were trying to suffocate me until I didn't know the truth about anything anymore.

"Since you've been here, you've convinced everyone that you're an air elemental," Nicole pointed out. "You don't have to *hide* your magic. You just have to continue blending in."

"Like how moving metal objects with my mind can look like I'm using air to control them," I said. "Except I can move metal swords and not wooden swords. How am I supposed to explain things like that?"

"Easy," Blake said. "Just pretend you suck at all of it."

"But they all saw me use my magic in archery practice."

"Beginner's luck." He shrugged.

"Have you used your magic in front of anyone since the last time we talked here?" Kate asked.

"No."

"So other than the archery class, the only people who've seen you use your magic are Alyssa and Zane."

I sat straighter at the sound of his name.

Relax, I told myself, crossing my legs and taking what I hoped came across as a calm, steady breath. I couldn't act weird when they mentioned him. If I acted weird, then—

"You two are a thing, aren't you?" Nicole asked.

"What?" I shook myself out of my thoughts. "No."

Her eyes twinkled with amusement. She didn't believe me.

But maybe she was onto something. Because if I was somewhat honest about my feelings for Zane, it would explain why I tensed up whenever he was mentioned. It could keep them from digging further into him and possibly uncovering his secret.

The best lies were based on the truth… right?

"I don't know," I admitted. "I like him. But only sometimes. Because he's kind of an asshole. So… that's kind of where things are at between us right now."

"Do you think he'd say anything about the magic you used to melt the deadbolt on his door? And on the knife to distract the handmaiden?" Kate asked.

"No," I said quickly.

He wouldn't reveal my secrets, since the one I had on him was so much bigger.

But of course, I couldn't tell them that.

"He's not the gossiping type," I said simply, since I

needed some sort of explanation for trusting him despite my declaration that he was an asshole. Not the best reason, but it could work.

"He does seem pretty reserved," Kate said. "As for Alyssa..."

She didn't need to say any more.

We all knew why Alyssa wouldn't be spreading my secrets anytime soon. I'd visited her today, and while she hadn't gotten worse, she hadn't gotten better, either.

But the longer she remained stable, the more time my mom had to figure out how to heal her.

My mom. *Hecate.*

I didn't think I was ever going to get used to that. It was like the person I knew as my mom was gone, and a stranger had taken her place.

My heart grieved for the version of her I'd known.

"I can definitely pretend I'm terrible at using my magic. It's a good idea," I said, and the others looked content with my response.

After all, what was another lie on top of all the others?

CHAPTER SIX

After dinner, I returned to my room and found myself once again staring at the texts from Zane.

He'd been quiet all day.

But after my conversation with the others in the cottage, I needed to talk to him. I had to make sure he wouldn't tell anyone the truth about my magic.

It was almost midnight, but I had a feeling he'd be awake.

Want to talk? I typed out.

I pressed send, figuring it was best to keep it simple and not overthink anything.

His response came nearly instantly.

Where?

Somewhere private, I wrote.

I know just the place. Meet me at the dock in fifteen minutes?

Sure, I replied. *Sounds good.*

I put on my winter layers in less than ten minutes, which was a great achievement given that thanks to the Florida weather, I'd never owned a pair of long johns until a few weeks ago. Once satisfied that I had enough layers on that I wouldn't freeze to death, I hurried out of the dorm and headed to the lake.

Zane was waiting at the end of the dock. His hair and skin glistened in the moonlight, like he was meant to live in the night. He kept his ice-blue eyes locked on mine as I walked toward him, quickly at first, but then more hesitantly as the pull I felt while around him took hold.

I stopped when I was a few feet away from him.

"You came," he said.

"Yeah." I stared up at him, breathless. Then, realizing I must sound like a vapid idiot, I added, "I was the one who reached out to you."

"I knew you'd break eventually."

He sounded so sure about it that I wanted to knock that amused smile off his face. But I restrained myself.

Barely.

"I didn't *break*," I said. "I needed answers."

"Good. Because I want to give them to you." He motioned to one of the wooden rowboats tied to the dock. "We can take it out to talk in private."

"The lake is frozen over," I stated the obvious.

I guessed the freeze had happened so quickly that they

hadn't had time to put away the boats, because the ice had hardened around their bottoms, trapping them.

He shook his head slightly, like I was being ridiculous, then casually stepped into the boat and sat down. "Don't you trust me?" he asked, like it was a challenge.

"Absolutely not."

"Yet you came out to talk to me because you wanted answers. You wouldn't be here if you didn't think I'd give you truthful ones."

He turned to face the front of the boat, leaned over, and pressed his palm against the ice. It melted under his touch, freeing the boat, and traveled outward to the center of the lake. The path was wide enough that we'd be able to row the oars, and the water was so dark that it *looked* cold—like it was waiting for someone to fall in so it could pull them under and never let them go.

He turned to me, his eyes serious. "You're safe with me," he said, holding his hand out to help me into the boat. "I promise."

I crossed my arms over my chest and glanced around uneasily. "Why can't you just tell me here?"

"Would you believe me if I said I wanted to take you on a romantic boat ride on the frozen lake?"

He looked so genuine that I wanted to say yes.

"The last time you tried to do something romantic for me, we were attacked and almost killed in the woods," I said instead.

"We weren't 'almost killed,'" he said, like the notion was ridiculous. "She never stood a chance against us."

"But she *tried* to kill us."

Still, I stared at his hand, a thrill running up my spine at the thought of my skin touching his. Zane had this air about him that made everything seem like an adventure. It was exciting.

Deceptively so.

What if this was a trap so he could push me into the lake and drown me under the ice to make sure the truth of what he really was stayed buried forever?

"Never mind." He leaned back over the side of the boat and touched the water, turning it back to ice. It was the exact same as before—no one would have ever known it had been tampered with. "Do you want to go back to my room? You look cold."

A tempting proposition.

But a dangerous one. Because I wasn't sure I trusted myself alone in his room with him.

"Here's fine," I said quickly—maybe a little *too* quickly.

"Cool." He got out of the boat and sat at the end of the dock, his feet dangling off the edge over the ice.

I joined him, making sure to put at least a foot of space between us.

He watched me like I was a goddess, and my heart warmed under his caring gaze.

Maybe I was easily deceived, but I couldn't believe that someone who looked at me the way Zane currently was would ever wish me harm, let alone be the one to cause it.

"So," he started. "What do you want to know?"

Everything.

But that was too broad. I needed to start with a pointed question.

"You said you're an immortal," I said. "How old are you really?"

I braced myself for him to say something creepy, like a hundred or a thousand years old.

"Twenty-one," he said. "Well, technically I've been around for over ten thousand years. But my people—the few of us who were still alive after Ragnarök—were buried in the ice when I was seventeen. We were only released four years ago. So, I've only been consciously alive for twenty-one of those years."

I stared at him as I tried to sort through that in my head.

"Are you okay?" he asked.

"Yeah," I said. "That was just... a lot."

"I know. I'll stay as long as you want and answer any questions you have."

"Okay," I said, still trying to organize my spinning thoughts. "What's Ragnarök?"

I'd heard it mentioned before, and I'd read about it a bit in the scrolls, but I didn't know much.

"It was the battle between the immortals and the gods," he said. "The *Norse* gods."

"And they won?"

"No. They killed most of us, and we killed most of them. Then the Great Flood washed all of us away."

"You mean the flood from the Old Testament? The one where Noah survived in the ark with the animals?"

"That's the one."

"Wow," I said. "That was... a long time ago."

"It was," he said. "The last thing I remember was being surrounded by water so deep that it was impossible to swim out, and it turning to ice around me."

"But how could you get trapped in the ice?" I asked. "You have ice magic."

"Stronger magic than ours exists out there," he said. "It was a cruel trick—trapping us with an element we can usually control."

"Who trapped you?"

"We don't know." He shrugged and gazed out at the frozen lake. "We also don't know who brought us back. We have our theories, but we don't know for sure."

We were both silent for a minute as I tried to process this.

"It must have been scary," I finally said. "The last thing you knew was the world before the flood. Then you woke up to *this.*" I motioned at the school behind us. "It must have been like waking up on an alien planet."

"It certainly took some adjustment." The way he said it made it sound far simpler than I imagined it must have been. "But the state of the world when we woke wasn't our biggest surprise."

"Oh?" I waited for him to elaborate.

"The biggest surprise was finding out that our world was being ruled by false gods." He watched me intensely as he said it, and realization of what he meant clicked.

"You mean the Greek gods."

"Yes," he said. "They came into existence after we were locked away, and they stole what was ours. But now we've returned, and we're going to take it back."

CHAPTER SEVEN

His eyes gleamed hard with determination, and I froze at how intensely he spoke.

As if he were out for blood.

"You want to kill the Greek gods," I said, trying to wrap my mind about it. "And you're starting here—at the academy?"

"The academy is full of the strongest descendants and children of the gods," he said. "Killing their offspring is a good way to get their attention."

"But you saved me," I said.

"I did."

"Why?"

"I already told you. I saved you because you're my soulmate."

At the word, frustration rushed through my body. "What does that even mean?" I asked.

"Immortals all have soulmates," he said. "We don't know why, but the theory is that experiencing such intense love for someone else keeps us grounded."

"You mean it keeps you human."

"My people existed long before humans. And before the gods—both the Norse and Greek," he said. "But yes—it deepens our conscience."

"And you think I'm your soulmate."

"I don't *think* you are," he said. "I *know* you are."

He stared at me so intensely that it took my breath away.

I needed to change the subject. Now. Before I became too distracted by the energy pulling me toward him to continue this conversation.

"So, you and Vera are here to spy on us and kill us," I said, feeling strangely detached as I said it. Like this was happening to other people—not to me and those I'd come to care about. "But why send the handmaidens to do it? Why not do it yourselves?"

He tilted his head slightly, sizing me up. "I never mentioned Vera."

"But I'm right, aren't I?" I asked. "She's an immortal, too?"

"Her secrets aren't mine to tell."

"So, yes. She *is* an immortal."

He remained silent, which I took as a yes.

"And does she know about me?" I asked.

"Not yet."

I let out a breath, which was visible in the cold air. "Good," I said. "The last thing I need is for her to hate me more than she already does."

"If Vera learns the truth about our connection, she'll be sympathetic to you," he said confidently. "She'll understand that you're one of us now."

"What makes you so sure of that?"

"Do you remember what I told you about how her boyfriend died in a car accident a few years ago?" he asked.

"Of course."

"That wasn't exactly the truth."

"Okay," I said slowly. "So, what *is* the truth?"

"There was no car accident," he said. "Vera's 'boyfriend' was her soulmate. When we were released from the ice, he wasn't there. He didn't survive Ragnarök. Her soul is forever broken because of it. She understands the intensity of a soulmate bond."

"But it sounds like her boyfriend was one of you," I said. "An immortal."

"He was."

"So, do immortals typically develop this bond with someone who isn't immortal?"

I couldn't bring myself to say the word.

Soulmate.

"Usually," he said. "Although there have been a few

times when a soulmate connection occurred with one of us and a god."

"But the immortals and the Norse gods want to start a war with the Greeks," I continued.

"No."

"But you just said..."

"I said the immortals are going to take back what's ours," he said. "It was ours before the Norse gods, and before the Greek gods. We existed before all of them."

"You want to kill me and everyone I love." The words felt hollow, as if it couldn't possibly be true.

"Not you," he said. "Our soulmate bond makes you one of us. My people and I will protect you."

I scooted away from him, horrified. "What about all the others?" I asked. "Alyssa? Jamie? Nicole? Blake? Kate? My mom?"

"They'll have to accept the immortals as their rightful rulers," he said. "Those who do will live. The others..."

He didn't have to say it.

They'd die.

Of course, this was assuming the immortals could accomplish what they were setting out to do.

"And why do you think I won't go to Kate and turn you in right now?" I asked.

"Because of this." Faster than humanly possible, he moved toward me, and his lips were on mine.

They were ice-cold, but heat flared through my body. I

couldn't think. I could barely breathe. All I could do was lean into him, my heart pounding as he tangled his fingers in my hair, pulling me closer.

My body reacted to his in a way my mind knew it shouldn't.

His kiss became hungrier—greedier—and my heart leaped with excitement. I wanted this. I *needed* this.

Then, flashes of the people I'd mentioned earlier appeared in my mind.

Alyssa. Jamie. Nicole. Blake. Kate. My mom.

The people Zane said the immortals wanted to destroy.

"No." I pushed him away, shaking myself out of his spell. "I can't do this. Not with you. You're a…"

But as I looked into his caring eyes, I couldn't say it.

Monster.

His beauty was deceiving. But at the end of the day, he and his people were monsters set out to destroy the gods and take over the world. If they succeeded, who knew what they'd do from there?

And why would my soul ever be connected to his?

I stood and wiped the cold, minty taste of him from my lips. "I don't want your protection," I said. "And I don't want to keep your secret."

"The barriers are still up around the school," he said coolly—calmly. "They keep everyone out—and in. Me and Vera included. We're strong, but not strong enough to go up against an entire school full of supernaturals. If you tell them the truth, they'll kill us."

"It sounds like they should," I said darkly.

His eyes flashed with betrayal. "You don't mean that."

I wanted to say that I did.

Except he was right—I didn't mean it. Because at the end of the day, Zane had protected me against the handmaiden. He'd killed her. He'd turned on her *for me*.

He cared about me. And I didn't want to turn my back on him.

At least not yet.

"I've gotta go," I said, and then I spun around and hurried up the dock, not looking back.

CHAPTER EIGHT

Between thinking about everything Zane had said at the lake and looking at photos of me and my mom to search for hints of her true identity, sleeping that night proved impossible.

How was I supposed to sleep when it felt like my world was shattering around me?

I was a zombie through my morning classes. I didn't hear a word of what my teachers were saying. I didn't take any notes, either.

Five minutes before lunch, my watch buzzed with a text from Nicole.

Come to the infirmary ASAP.

It was about Alyssa. It had to be.

Was she awake? Had she worsened?

Once class was dismissed, I shoved my laptop into my bag and hurried to the door—nearly running two other students over in the process.

"You okay?" Jamie was by my side in a second, since we always walked to the dining hall together.

"I have to go to the library," I said the first excuse that popped into my mind. "I totally forgot about something I have due tomorrow."

She studied me suspiciously. "Okay," she said slowly. "I'll see you in training."

I practically ran the entire way to the library.

Nicole was in the waiting room, arguing with two people I'd only seen in photos until now—Alyssa's parents. Unlike Alyssa, they were tall and regal. Her mom shared Alyssa's blonde hair, and she wore a huge fur jacket that looked expensive. And her dad's long trench coat made him look more British than American.

The door clicked shut behind me, and the three of them looked to me and silenced.

"Summer," Nicole said my name in relief, and then she looked back at Alyssa's parents. "This is Alyssa's suitemate. Summer Donovan."

Alyssa's mom sized me up, not looking impressed. "The new girl who got her magic after the semester started," she said in distaste, her lips pursed like she'd just eaten something sour.

"Hi." I shuffled uneasily. Alyssa's parents seemed to be just as snobby as she'd warned. "What's going on?

How's Alyssa doing?" I glanced at the door that led to her room.

"We're here to bring our daughter home," her dad said, his tone firm and no-nonsense.

"You mean she's awake?" I bounced on my toes, eager to see her.

"Her condition hasn't changed," he said, and my excitement deflated. "From what I understand, it's not going to. So, we've made arrangements to bring her safely home, where she belongs."

No.

I felt the word deep in my bones. Alyssa would prefer to be here—not at her home. And her parents hated the academy. I had a feeling that if they took her away, she'd never return.

"She has to stay here," I said quickly. "She's safe here."

Alyssa's mom raised a thinly plucked eyebrow in disdain. "You truly think she's safest in the place that caused her to end up like this?"

"The boundaries are stronger now," Nicole insisted. "She's safe."

"Well, excuse me if her condition makes me skeptical of that," her mom said.

"The boundaries *will* protect her," I said. "And we're going to figure out a way to heal her. When we do, she needs to be here. It's what she'd want."

"You've known my daughter for what—two weeks?"

her mom asked, and I pressed my lips together, since it was true. "You have no clue what she wants, let alone what she needs. None of you do." She glared at Nicole, as if this were her fault. "The only one whose magic can help her now is our true goddess—Hecate."

My mom.

I didn't think I'd ever get used to it.

"Hecate's magic," I repeated, an idea coming to me. "You should use it."

"What are you talking about?" Her mom regarded me as if I was officially crazy.

"You practice tarot, right?" I already knew the answer —Alyssa had learned how to read tarot from her mom.

Her mom's eyes narrowed. They were the same blue as Alyssa's, but they were dull compared to Alyssa's sparkle. "Yes." She straightened her shoulders, haughty in her fur coat. "I'm well-versed in the art of reading the cards."

"And you believe the cards are connected to Hecate's magic?"

She paused for a second. "I see my daughter's been teaching you things outside your assigned curriculum."

I couldn't tell for sure, but from the way the side of her lip twitched slightly upward, I'd say she was pleased.

"I don't know how to read the cards," I said, although given that I'd literally been *raised by Hecate*, I probably should have mastered them by now. "But you trust

Hecate's magic to help heal Alyssa. Maybe you could do a tarot reading to see if you should keep Alyssa here or bring her back home?"

She pursed her lips together, silent again.

Could she actually be considering it?

"Very well. We'll consult Hecate." She reached into her tote bag and pulled out a small box sized perfectly to fit tarot cards. "If you'll excuse us, we're going to return to my daughter's room. *In private.*" She all but hissed as she said the last two words. Then she spun around, her coat swirling behind her, and let herself into Alyssa's room.

Her husband followed, shutting the door before I could peek in.

"Well." Nicole released a long breath. "That went better than I expected."

"Why'd you text *me* to come?" I asked.

"Instinct." She shrugged. "Plus, you're far tougher and intimidating than you realize. I think it must be the whole 'daughter of you-know-who' aura you give off."

Hades.

She obviously couldn't say his name in public. So apparently, we'd talk about him as if he were Voldemort.

"It sort of worked," she continued. "So, what do you think? Are they actually going to do that tarot reading, or are they going to lie so they can bring Alyssa home?"

"From what Alyssa's told me, her parents are true

followers of Hecate," I said. "But they're also total snobs, as you just saw."

"I take it she doesn't get along well with them?"

"That's an understatement." At that, I thought about my own mom. Because we'd always gotten along well. I'd always appreciated our relationship and been grateful for it.

But now, knowing how much she'd lied to me…

"No matter what, at least you tried," Nicole interrupted my train of thought. "Now, I guess we just wait."

"Yeah."

We sat down, and I played with the tips of my fingers, anxiously waiting for Alyssa's parents to come back out.

Eventually, they emerged. They were both frowning, and their eyes looked sad. Her father more than her mother.

Nicole was instantly on her feet.

I got up slower—more hesitantly.

"What happened?" Nicole asked.

Alyssa's mom's eyes zeroed in on me. "As I mentioned earlier, I have faith in Hecate," she started. "We consulted the cards. Multiple times. It appears that the best thing for Alyssa is to stay at the academy."

I hadn't realized how tight my chest had been feeling until after she'd spoken.

"So, she'll be staying here?" I asked.

"For now. But if there isn't any progress in her condition by the next moon cycle, we'll be taking her home."

"Okay." I looked to Nicole for guidance. "We can do that."

I just needed to trust that my mom would get answers about how to cure Norse injuries by then, and that the cards wouldn't have given them this advice if it wasn't possible.

"Now, if the two of you don't mind, we'd like some time alone with our daughter," Alyssa's dad said.

"Of course," I said. "And thank you."

"Don't thank us," her mom said. "Thank Hecate."

With that, she turned around, and she and her husband went back inside Alyssa's room and slammed the door shut behind them.

CHAPTER NINE

For the next three days, I successfully avoided Zane. What he'd told me the other night was a lot to process. I couldn't even write my feelings down in my journal, for fear of someone finding it. Instead, the emotions were a storm of confusion inside me, and I had no idea what to do with them.

But I couldn't avoid him forever, since this morning, Kate had called for an all-school assembly in the theatre.

I sat near the back with the rest of the air students.

Zane was also in the back, although he was at the far corner. Of course, he was sitting next to Vera. They both looked stone-cold and devoid of emotions.

I focused on chit-chatting with Jamie so Zane wouldn't catch me staring at him.

Eventually, Kate walked onto the stage, and everyone silenced.

"I'm sure you're wondering why I called you all here today," she said. "Especially since it's a Sunday."

Various murmurs of "yes," echoed through the theatre.

"The academy has been through a lot these past few weeks," she continued, and everyone silenced again as sadness blanketed the room. "I think it would be good for us to get our minds off everything, to potentially lift our spirits. Which is why I—along with the rest of the staff—have decided to host Greek Week early this year."

Some students whooped in excitement—mostly ones sitting around me. Air students. The fire students sounded happy as well.

Zane and Vera appeared neutral.

Did immortals even *have* the same level of emotions as us? Or were their hearts as cold as their magic?

Kate raised her hands for everyone to be quiet, and they all settled down. "The competition will begin tomorrow. And unlike previous years, all academic classes will be cancelled this week so you can double-up on your training. It will be exhausting—both mentally and physically—but I believe every person sitting in this room is up for the task."

The only students who looked bummed about academic classes being cancelled were the earth students.

"When we get back, I'm going to need you to tell me what Greek Week is," I murmured to Jamie.

Her eyes widened in surprise, then understanding. "Don't worry," she said. "I'll tell you *everything.*"

"All right." Jamie sat on the small couch in my room, and she pressed her fingers together to make a small teepee with her hands. "Greek Week."

"I have a feeling we won't be sitting around learning how to speak Greek," I joked as I made myself comfortable on my bed.

"No." She scrunched her nose in horror. "That sounds awful."

"It does," I agreed.

"Greek Week is a competition," she started. "Of both magic abilities and physical skill. The dorms compete against each other."

"Like quidditch?"

"No, it's not a team competition," she said. "It's individual. Think Hunger Games, but without killing each other. And more organized."

"But you just said the dorms compete against each other."

"They do," she said. "Each dorm will pick a champion. That'll happen tomorrow."

"How do we pick a champion?" I asked.

"Easy." She smiled mischievously. "We face off against each other until only one of us is left standing."

"Got it," I said, and the thrill of competition flooded my veins.

Except I needed to pretend I was terrible at using my magic, to keep all eyes off me.

"I have a pretty good feeling I'll be knocked out in round one," I said lightly. "Since I just started here and all."

"You don't have to compete if you don't want to," she said. "It's on a volunteer-only basis."

"Are you gonna do it?"

"I'd like to." She twirled a strand of her hair around her finger, looking anxious. "The seniors and juniors wouldn't be happy about it, but we've never had a freshman air dorm champion before. It would be cool to be the first."

"If you do, you know I'll be rooting for you from the sidelines." I gave her an encouraging smile.

"Thanks," she said, although she quickly brushed it off. "But choosing our champion is only day one. After that are the face-off rounds. Two champions will face off on Tuesday, and the other two on Wednesday. It's a random draw about which dorms compete against each other first."

"Got it," I said. "And then the winners of the face-off rounds compete on Thursday?"

"You're a quick study." She moved closer to the edge of the couch in excitement. "But Greek Week doesn't end there. It wouldn't be complete without the celebration ball on Friday night."

"You mean a school dance?"

"You say that like it's a bad thing."

"I'm guessing you've never stood at the wall during a middle school dance because the guys won't get within a five-foot radius of you." I frowned, since those were memories I preferred to forget.

"That won't happen at this ball," she said confidently. "Firstly, we don't have to deal with humans who are intimidated by us. Secondly, everyone goes with dates. Like at prom. You *did* go to prom, right?"

I took a deep breath and leaned back into my pillow, since prom was another one of those things I liked to try erasing from my memory.

"Only because my best friend forced me," I said. "She was dating a guy from another school, and she set me up on a blind date with one of his friends. He ended up leaving with another girl."

"Wow." She widened her eyes in surprise. "That's cold."

"Tell me about it."

"Don't worry—there are lots of guys here who I'm sure will ask you," she said. "I'll make sure you have a good time."

Lara had promised she'd make sure I had a good time at prom as well. But maybe things *would* be better this time, since like Jamie had pointed out, I was with others who were like me.

Sort of like me. Because no one else here was a daughter of Hades. Which was apparently enough to make me intimidating even to other witches.

But not to Zane.

The unwelcome thought flashed into my mind, and I did my best to push it away. Because even if he asked—which I suspected he might do—no way on Earth would I go with him.

"What're you thinking about?" Jamie asked, zapping me out of my thoughts.

I glanced at the door that led to the bathroom I shared with Alyssa. "Just that I wish Alyssa were here with us," I lied. "This ball sounds like something she'd love."

"She would," she agreed. "But there's always next year."

She tried to sound optimistic about it, but from the way her smile didn't reach her eyes, I knew she was worried.

And while I wanted to have faith that Alyssa would pull through, I was worried, too.

CHAPTER TEN

During breakfast in the dorm the next morning, I could already feel the competitive vibe in the air.

Eventually, all forty-three of us headed to the gym, where Mason waited for us in the center of the basketball court. He wore sweatpants, a white t-shirt transparent enough to show off his defined abs, and his dark hair was slicked back into a man-bun. His tan skin managed to glow supernaturally, even in the terrible lightning of the gym.

A table with a selection of wood training swords was behind him.

"Welcome to the sixth annual Greek Week." He eyed us, analyzing our potential. I could have sworn his eyes stopped for a second longer on me. "Take a seat in the bleachers. Seniors in the front row, juniors behind them, etcetera."

We made our way to the bleachers, and Jamie and I sat next to each other with the other freshmen.

Greg plopped down on Jamie's other side, his leg brushing hers.

She scooted closer to me.

Defeat crossed his eyes, and with his bronze curly hair, he looked like a lost puppy. But he straightened a second later, creating the perfect image of confidence. "So," he said. "Are you guys gonna compete?"

"Nope," I said, even though every bone in my body wanted to say *yes*. If I used the full strength of my powers, I might even have a chance of winning.

But these were just games—it wasn't a *real* fight. The only thing the winner got was being celebrated at the ball on Friday night.

Still, it didn't stop me from wanting to see how far my magic could take me.

Although there would be one big problem—the swords were made of wood, not metal. I wouldn't have a chance, anyway.

"I'm thinking about it." Jamie shrugged. "It can't hurt to try."

"Besides the fact that the seniors and juniors will be *pissed*," Greg said.

"Oh well." Jamie was too focused on checking out Mason to give Greg any attention beyond that.

The seniors and juniors were talking excitedly

amongst themselves, with Lincoln Howe in the center. A descendent of Zeus, he was a blond, sculpted, gregarious senior who everyone assumed would win. From the relaxed, confident way he chatted back with them, he seemed to assume he was going to win, too.

"Today, we'll determine which one of you will represent the air dorm in Greek Week." Mason's voice boomed through the gym, and everyone silenced. "You'll face off against each other until only one of you is left standing, and that person will be our champion. This will be on a volunteer-only basis—no one will be forced to compete, although if your magic is powerful, it's highly encouraged."

His eyes *definitely* went to me at that part.

I held his gaze for a moment, and from his amused smirk, I could practically hear him asking me to volunteer. But I looked down at my hands, reminding myself of my promise to Blake and the others.

Stay under the radar.

"We're starting with the seniors." Mason studied the students in the front row. "Who wants to go first?"

Nearly all of their hands went up.

"Lincoln and Zenon," he decided, and he moved to stand closer to the bleachers. "You're up."

An interesting match-up, given that Zenon—with her tiny frame and short blonde hair—looked like she'd be smoked by Lincoln.

They each chose a wooden sword befitting their size and strode to the center of the basketball court. They held their swords at the ready, eyes locked, looking ready to draw blood.

"Remember—we're here to spar, not to truly injure each other," Mason reminded them. "First one to land a blow to the neck or heart wins."

He counted to three, blew his whistle, and the fight began.

Lincoln tackled Zenon in less than fifteen seconds, pinned her to the ground, and held his sword at her neck. He didn't even use an ounce magic—he was just a beast at swordplay.

"Pinned you—again," he said to her, and from the way her eyes narrowed, I had a feeling there was history between them. Then he let out a victorious roar and raised his sword in triumph. "And *that's* how it's done." He stared down the others on the bleachers, daring them to try going up against him.

"Well done, Lincoln," Mason said. "Come stand next to me. Zenon, return to your seat on the bleachers."

The small girl pulled herself up and hurried back to her seat. The guy next to her told her she did a good job, even though it was clearly a lie.

All twelve seniors faced off against each other, until the six losers were sent back to the bleachers, and the six winners stood next to Mason. Then the winners faced off again, until three remained.

Lincoln, a follower of his named William, and a girl named Penny who preferred to fight defensively instead of offensively.

"The final three." Mason smirked, amused. He seemed *constantly* amused—as if the world was one big joke, and each person in it a pawn in his game. "You know how this works. You'll all fight at once until only one's left standing."

They strode to the center and raised their swords to face off. Lincoln gave William a simple, short, "macho male" nod, and William acknowledged it in return. It was like they'd had a short conversation without actually speaking.

Mason blew the whistle, and the guys rushed at Penny.

Penny dodged them easily, keeping her sword firmly in hand.

The guys kept trying to run her down, but she used her size to her advantage, continuing to dodge their attempted blows.

Her eyes gleamed with determination, and she ran at William and jumped, flying toward him with air at her heels. In one fell swoop, she disarmed him and caught his neck with the side of her sword.

"William is out!" Mason said, and William returned to the bleachers.

Penny and Lincoln circled each other like wolves about to attack.

He bared his teeth and ran at her, and like a gymnast, she jumped and flipped over his sword. A breeze rushed through the air—she'd pulled off that maneuver with the help of magic. This continued a few more times, and growing anger swirled in Lincoln's eyes, his face red with rage.

She was baiting him, and his fury was a physical thing I could feel in the air. Judging by how the others had silenced and were sitting on the edges of their seats as well, they felt the same.

Suddenly, Lincoln dropped his sword down to his feet, screamed, and blasted a gust of wind at Penny so strong that it sent her flying to the back of the gym. She smacked into the wall and collapsed in a heap on the floor.

Lincoln rushed over to her, picked up her fallen sword, and slammed the tip of it on her chest with far more force than necessary. He was heaving with exertion, and sweat dripped from his face onto the floor.

She stirred, and he kept his sword pointed at her heart.

It was so silent that it sounded like Lincoln was the only one breathing.

Mason started clapping slowly. "Congratulations, Lincoln!" he said. "You're the victor of the senior class.

Come stand next to me. Zenon, you can escort Penny to the infirmary."

Zenon rushed over to Penny, whispering quietly to her as she helped her up.

Penny sent a seething glance at Lincoln. "I'm fine," she said, although by how difficult it was for her to force the words out, I doubted it was true. "I can stay."

"As you wish." Mason motioned to the bleachers, and Penny hobbled over to them with Zenon's help.

The juniors faced off next, and then the sophomores. Only two sophomores volunteered to compete—probably because Lincoln was glaring at them like he was looking forward to murdering them.

"Next up—freshmen." Mason looked to our row. "Are any of you daring enough to have a go?"

Lincoln cracked his knuckles so loudly that each pop echoed through the gym.

No one raised their hands.

Mason opened his mouth to say something, but Jamie stood before he could.

"I am," she said, sounding strong and confident.

Lincoln gave her a death glare, but she didn't back down.

Mason smirked in approval. "We need at least one more freshman to volunteer for you to face off against, so you can qualify for the next round. Any takers?"

No one volunteered.

"I see you're forcing my hand. So, I'll pick one of you at random." Mason's gaze instantly went to me. "Summer Donovan. Face off against Jamie to see which one of you will proceed to the next round."

I scowled at him. "I thought no one could be forced to volunteer?" I asked, although as I said it, the urge to compete rushed through me again.

The urge to prove I was stronger than they thought. Especially Lincoln, who was grinning at me like I was fresh meat, his sharp teeth ready to chow down on me.

"I'm not *forcing* you to do anything." Mason's eyes twinkled mischievously. "I'm offering you the opportunity to give your friend a chance to advance in the competition."

I steadied my breathing, saying nothing.

"I'll do it," Greg said quickly.

"The time to volunteer is over," Mason snapped. "It's Jamie versus Summer, or nothing."

Greg curled his fingers to make a fist. "That's not an actual rule."

"I'm in charge here," Mason said. "I make the rules. But don't worry—it's simply a formality, since Summer has the least training out of all of you. If she agrees to compete, Jamie will be a shoo-in to proceed to the next round."

Really? He was volunteering me because he was *that* confident I'd lose?

"Come on, Summer." Jamie's eyes widened, begging me. "Let me do this."

I frowned. Because apparently Jamie assumed I'd lose, too. Or maybe she thought I'd hand the competition over to her, since I wasn't the one who wanted this?

It was what I *should* do. It was the perfect opportunity to show everyone how "terrible" I was at my magic.

But Lincoln was still baring his teeth at me. And anger formed in my throat at the memory of how he'd thrown Penny into the wall and slammed her so hard with the sword that I was surprised the impact hadn't stopped her heart.

I was close to positive that I could take him down.

But I couldn't do it with wooden practice swords.

"Fine." I shot Lincoln a death glare of my own, then returned my focus to Mason. "But only if we use real swords."

CHAPTER ELEVEN

Mason grinned, looking like as much of a predator as Lincoln. "This just got far more exciting than I anticipated." He pointed his palm toward the back of the gym, and a cart with metal swords rolled onto the basketball court. "Luckily for you, I plan for anything."

Jamie glared down at me. "Why did you do that?" she asked.

I tensed, since obviously I couldn't tell her the real reason. "I thought you wanted to show that freshmen should be taken seriously?"

"By *winning*," she hissed. "Not by doing… whatever you're trying to do."

"It's too late to change your minds now," Mason said. "You either fight with real swords until first blood is drawn, or forfeit. What will it be?"

He was getting such a kick out of this that I wanted to smack that arrogant smirk off his face.

"We'll fight." I regarded Jamie sternly, so she'd go along with it. It wasn't like I was going to actually hurt her. The fight was until first blood, so a small cut would do the trick.

"Sure." Jamie shook off her surprise and marched to the center circle. From the determined look in her eyes, I could tell she knew that I wasn't in this anymore to let her win so she could progress to the next round. "Let's go."

I positioned myself across from her, steadied my stance, and held my sword at the ready. The magic from the metal flowed through my palms, tingling as it made its way through my veins. My mind latched onto the sword—and to the one in Jamie's hand.

I could snatch it away from her before she'd understand what was happening.

But that would draw suspicion to my magic. I needed to go about this correctly. And since I'd already mentally committed to truly doing this, I'd have to make it look like my metal magic was actually air magic.

I could do this. I *had* to do it, or I'd risk being dragged into the Underworld and imprisoned there for who knew how long.

No, a voice of reason crossed my mind. This was dumb. I should just let Jamie win and stay off the radar for the rest of Greek Week.

But then Mason smirked arrogantly, and Lincoln sneered at me, and anger rushed through me again. Because I wasn't weak. And I refused to let those two jerks put me "in my place."

I'd been stuck on the sidelines for all my life—ignored by most everyone around me. I was *not* about to back down now. Besides, I'd been using my metal magic since starting at the academy, and no one had kidnapped me to the Underworld yet.

As long as I was smart about it, it was going to be fine.

"One," Mason started counting off. "Two. Three."

He blew his whistle.

Jamie charged and brought her sword down on me, but I blocked her blow, the sound of metal against metal clanging in the air.

She glared at me, and the expression in her eyes was clear.

Game on.

But I was so in tune with both the weapon in her hand and the one in mine that she couldn't get a strike in.

This was how I'd do it. Continue blocking her attacks —make it look like I was a natural at sword fighting. Tire her out. Then I'd make my move. Like how Penny had fought defensively, but better.

I used the space of the gym to my advantage, running around it as Jamie continued to attack. My physical fitness hadn't been the greatest thing in the world before starting at the academy, but after a few weeks of training, I'd already seen a huge improvement.

Thanks to the wind at her heels, Jamie was fast. But eventually, she started slowing down. Her cheeks were pink, and she was sweating up a storm.

Just what I wanted.

I cornered her, and she ran at me with so much ferocity that she let out an angry scream. But I latched onto her sword with my mind, snatching it out of her grip so it fell to the ground.

I used her moment of shock to slice a small cut along her arm.

A drop of blood fell to the floor beside her sword.

We both froze, our eyes on her blood.

The students in the bleachers cheered.

When she looked back up at me, she was pissed. "I don't know what you just did, but you're going to tell me later," she said, quietly enough that the others across the gym wouldn't have been able to hear her over their clapping.

"Congratulations, Summer!" Mason said. "The victor of the freshman class. Jamie, take a seat. Summer, come stand over here with me and the others."

Jamie gave me one last curious look, and we both walked to our spots.

Lincoln studied me like I was a bug he was dying to squash.

Mason retrieved Jamie's fallen sword, and he smiled down at it as he sauntered back, a dangerous expression in his eyes. "I must say—I like this idea of using actual swords," he said when he was back at my side. "It makes this much more exciting. So, we're going to continue using them for the final face-offs."

"Perfect." Lincoln's hungry gaze remained zeroed in on me.

Fire flooded my veins. I couldn't wait to eat him alive.

The final face-offs started with Lincoln against the victor of the junior class. The junior put up a good fight, but in the end, Lincoln was victorious.

The cut on her side bled so much that another student had to bring her to the infirmary. It wasn't lethal, but it also wasn't pretty.

I faced off against the sophomore victor next, using the same strategy I had with Jamie. It took longer to tire her out, but eventually, I succeeded. And just like I had with Jamie, I made sure the cut I gave her was as small as possible.

Next up—me against Lincoln. Which sort of wasn't fair, since Lincoln had time to rest between his fight with the junior and his fight with me, and I had to fight back-to-back.

Then again, "fairness" wouldn't come into play in a real battle. I intended to beat Lincoln, and it would put him in his place even *more* knowing that he'd had time to rest and I didn't.

Satisfaction buzzed through me at the thought.

But I was getting ahead of myself. Because I hadn't won yet.

Everyone in the bleachers was silent as Lincoln and I marched to the circle, stood across from each other, and raised our swords. I felt slightly winded from all that running around to tire out Jamie and the sophomore, but the sword's metal energized me.

Lincoln growled at me.

He was animalistic—impulsive. All brawn and no brain.

I could use that against him. Because while he was intimidating, he would be prone to miscalculations. Once he made one, I'd strike.

"Are you ready to bleed?" he snarled.

I didn't flinch under his killer gaze. "No," I said, steady and in control.

This only made him narrow his eyes further. "Then I suggest you get ready," he said. "Quickly."

"Great advice," I said, not backing down. "Hopefully you're as good at taking it as you are at dishing it out."

Mason took a few steps forward. "It's time to quit this mental foreplay and get to the actual fighting," he said. "One, two…"

He blew his whistle.

Lincoln charged.

His obvious move.

I was already prepared with my sword to block his blow.

His face was right up against mine, his breath hot and suffocating as he used brute force to push his sword against mine. But I stood my ground not just with my sword, but with my mind.

It didn't matter how strong he was—he wasn't going to kill me with my own element.

The veins in his arms bulged. "You're stronger than you look," he said. "But don't worry. I'm ready to break you."

"Like hell you will."

I spun away, his sword missing me by inches, and he stumbled at my sudden move.

"You bitch," he said, and he ran at me again.

I easily dodged his blow. "Creative," I goaded him, and some of the students chuckled in the bleachers.

Good to know they weren't all on Team Lincoln.

He roared and sent a gust of air at me, like he'd done to Penny.

Just like Penny, I flew backward and hit the ground. I let my sword fly out of my hand, so it was ten feet away from me.

Lincoln ran at me, his sword raised above his head, ready to bring it down on me.

I held onto his sword with my mind to hold him back, called mine back into my hand, and its handle smacked into my palm. Then, in one fell swoop, I sliced his forearm and rolled out of the way, just before the tip of his sword whammed into the floor so hard that it left a dent on the laminated wood.

If I hadn't moved in time, his blade would have killed me. Well, not *me,* since the metal would have bounced off my skin. But it would have killed anyone else in my position.

He stared at the blood coming out of his arm in shock, pressing his palm against it to try to stop the bleeding.

Then he ran at me again.

He stopped mid-way there, like he'd slammed into an invisible wall.

Mason held his arm out, his palm facing Lincoln, using his air magic to hold the senior in place. "Enough," he said. "The final face-off is over."

"She cheated," Lincoln growled. "We need a rematch."

"How did she cheat?" Mason sounded unbothered.

"She… did something," he sputtered. "To my sword."

I smiled victoriously. "Are you referring to how I stopped your sword from spearing my heart?"

Lincoln stopped trying to get past Mason's invisible wall, his eyes narrowed in a way that made it obvious he wasn't buying it. "It wasn't normal," he said.

"Which part?" I asked playfully, refusing to let him or

anyone else see that I was worried about what he might say next. "Getting beaten by a freshman, or getting beaten by a girl? Oh wait—I know. How about that part when you tried to kill me in a fight that was supposed to be until first blood drawn?"

He continued giving me a death glare, not looking the slightest bit guilty. "I'm talking about whatever you did to my sword."

"I dodged your sword." I rolled my eyes, then looked at Mason. "Are you ready to call this?"

He smirked, his eyes glinted with amusement. "I most certainly am," he said. "Summer Donovan—you're the official winner of the competition, and therefore, the champion of the air dorm for this year's Greek Week. Congratulations. From what you just showed us, you'll represent our element well."

My breathing stopped for a second. Because was it just me, or did he say "our element" with a slight bit of snark?

"Thank you," I said, surprised by how calm I sounded. "I hope I will."

"I know you will. Now, it's time for you all to break for lunch." He turned to Lincoln again, and his smile turned menacing—dangerous. "Except for you. You're staying here. Because the two of us need to have a little chat."

CHAPTER TWELVE

Lincoln wasn't there when we got back from lunch. No one knew what had happened to him, and Mason didn't say a word.

We practiced controlling the air to our advantage, like Mason had done to hold Lincoln off from running at me. But it was a high-level skill. Penny was the best of all of us, but even her "air walls" only lasted a few seconds.

Mine were, of course, non-existent. I felt everyone's eyes on me every time I tried—and the disappointment radiating from them each time I failed.

Some champion I was proving myself to be.

I also knew that when Nicole, Blake, and Kate found out what had happened, they were going to be pissed.

I probably just should have let Jamie win.

But then I wouldn't have been able to see that stunned

look on Lincoln's face when I'd sliced his arm with my sword. He'd probably be the champion of the air elementals right now—not me.

So, I didn't regret a thing.

After training, I managed to get some alone time in my room to shower and unwind. But dinner was about to be served downstairs, and I was *hungry*. After so much training in one day, there was no way the peanut butter and bread I kept in my room was going to satisfy me.

Plus, I was the champion representing the air dorm in Greek Week. I wanted the air elementals to support me, which meant going down there and mingling with them instead of holing myself up in my room.

So, I changed into my favorite outfit—black jeans, a black top, a black leather jacket, and matching boots—and headed downstairs. The jacket was a bit extra for hanging around in the dorm, but I was their champion now. I wanted to look the part. Plus, all-black clothing had always been my mental armor.

I entered the dining room, and everyone silenced, stopped eating, and stared at me.

I looked to Jamie for help.

She was sitting off to the side with some of our friends, and she crossed her arms and sat back in her seat, sulking. She'd ignored me all afternoon while we trained, and now, she seemed just as salty as before.

I looked around the room, panicked. Because without Jamie and the others to sit with, who was I supposed to eat dinner with?

Much to my relief, Penny stood up and pranced over to me. Nicole had healed her during lunch, so she was walking normally now. "You were amazing this morning," she said. "You have no idea how satisfying it was to watch you kick Lincoln's ass."

All of the tension I'd been feeling a few seconds ago disappeared.

"It was my pleasure." I beamed. "And it was satisfying for me, too."

"I bet it was," she said. "Want to come sit with me and my friends? We've seen Greek Weeks before, so we can help you strategize."

I glanced at Jamie again—like I was asking her permission to sit at another table. But she refused to meet my eyes.

"Sure," I said to Penny. "That sounds great."

I went up to the buffet to get my food—it was Italian night, which was one of my favorites—and sat in the chair Penny had saved for me. I hadn't spent much time with the juniors and seniors before this, but judging from the way everyone at the table hung on Penny's every word, I was getting the impression that she was the queen bee around here.

I was more than happy to enjoy my food and let her do most of the talking. And right now, she and the others were instructing me on how I should fight an earth elemental, since I'd be facing off against their champion in two days.

Their champion was Topher—Jamie's boyfriend. Which was probably another reason why she was so sulky.

Hopefully she'd be open to chatting privately after dinner. The tension between us was putting me seriously on edge. If Alyssa were here, she'd probably act as a mediator. But she wasn't here, which meant it was on me.

We were almost done eating when Nicole burst into the dining room. Just like when I'd walked in, everyone stopped talking and looked at her.

Her gray eyes were laser focused on one person—me.

"We need to talk," she said. "Now."

My heart stopped. Because I'd never seen Nicole angry, and I was surprised at the darkness I felt emanating off her.

I shrugged apologetically at Penny, then got up and followed Nicole out of the dining room and up the stairs to my suite.

She didn't say a word until we were inside with the door closed.

I braced myself for the scolding I was sure she was about to give me.

"So." She looked me up and down, assessing me. "I hear you're this year's champion of the air dorm."

"I didn't mean to do it," I started, my throat tightening. "But Jamie wanted to compete, and then Mason volunteered me to fight against her, and he said Jamie wouldn't qualify if I didn't. And the senior who'd won—Lincoln—was being such a bully about it. Jamie wouldn't have stood a chance against him. And I didn't want him to be our champion. So I went up against him… and I won."

Nicole's eyes widened, like she'd been blasted by freezing cold air. "Whoa," she said. "Why don't you start from the beginning, but slower this time?" She walked over to the couch and sat down, her message clear—she was open to hearing my side of what had happened.

"Sure." I had so much energy racing through me that I didn't sit. Instead, I took a deep breath, pacing around as I explained what had happened in more detail.

She was silent as I spoke, only giving me the occasional nod to let me know she was listening. As hard as I tried, I couldn't get a read on her.

Once I was finished, I regarded her nervously, waiting for her reaction.

"Wow." She studied me in a way that almost looked approving. "That was all very interesting."

"You're not mad?" I braced myself to be yelled at, or *something* other than what she was currently doing.

"Not at all," she said. "I probably would have done the same thing in your position. Actually, I know I would have."

"Wow," I said, relaxing fully. "I thought you were gonna be pissed."

"You underestimate me." She smirked, and I remembered how much of a badass she'd been when she and Blake had first walked through the door of my apartment in Florida and killed that harpy. "Kate, on the other hand…"

"She's angry."

"Mason brought Lincoln to her office and told her everything. Lincoln wouldn't stop talking about how you did something with your magic that you shouldn't have been able to do. So yeah, she's angry."

"Right," I said, since I hadn't expected anything else. "What did she do with Lincoln?"

"She expelled him."

I sucked in a sharp breath. "Because he knew too much?"

"No," she said. "Because he tried to kill you in a sparring session. From Mason's account, Lincoln *would* have killed you if you hadn't rolled out of the way. Murdering other students—or attempting to murder them—is against school rules. Obviously. So, she expelled him."

"Wow," I said. "Good."

"But you're right—he does know too much," she

continued. "Luckily, no one's taking him seriously. He just sounds like a sore loser when he says you beat him because you 'did something weird with your magic.' And it doesn't sound like anyone else noticed. But you need to be careful from here on out. Because the rest of the face-offs happen in front of the entire school. If the next person you fight also says you did something strange with your magic, it's going to start looking suspicious. So, keep the metal magic under wraps. Got it?"

"If I do that, I'll lose."

"Then you'll lose." She shrugged. "You already did what you wanted by putting Lincoln in his place. And we don't want to raise any more suspicion. You need to let it go. Can you do that?"

"Sure," I said, even though the others had been so excited during dinner that I hated the thought of letting them down.

"You mean it?" she asked. "No more metal magic?"

"I can't help being in tune with my sword," I said. "And it'll look suspicious if I'm suddenly terrible at swordplay. But I won't use my metal magic on anything else. I promise."

"Good point about that looking suspicious," she said. "I'm sure the others will agree."

"Right," I said. "And there's another thing I haven't thought about…"

"What?" Nicole asked, but I was already removing one of the stud earrings from my ear.

I jammed it into my palm and sucked in a sharp breath, holding it as pain rushed through me. Then, slowly, I pulled the earring out of my hand, watching blood bubble on my skin.

"Why did you do that?" Nicole's eyes were wide.

"Because I didn't know if I could be injured by my own element, since that dagger bounced off my palm in the fight with Lin. Now I know I can. I just thought to myself that I was going to let it puncture my skin, and my body listened." My palm pulsed with pain, and I held it out to her. "Can you heal it?"

She took my hand in hers, and a calming warmth radiated into the injury. When she removed her hand, the mini-stab wound was gone. There wasn't even a scar.

"Glad we figured that out," I said, putting my earring back in my ear. "It would have been pretty difficult to lose the next face-off if I couldn't be cut with a blade."

"True." She looked down, deep in thought, then refocused on me. "Speaking of healing—any word from your mom?"

"She's sent a few texts to check in," I said. "Other than that, nothing."

"Hopefully that means she's onto something."

"Yeah." The thought of Alyssa lying on that bed in the

infirmary crossed my mind, and sadness squeezed my lungs. "Hopefully."

Both of us were silent for a few seconds.

"All right," she said, standing up. "I should go. I'm glad we had this chat."

"Wait," I said as she walked to the door, and she turned around, waiting for me to continue. "Does Kate totally hate me for doing this?"

"She's not happy. But don't worry—she'll forgive you."

"And Blake?" I asked.

"He never liked Lincoln. He's thrilled that you kicked his ass."

I smiled at that. "And what does he think about Topher?"

She tilted her head slightly, and I could swear she looked amused. "Does it matter?"

"Just curious." I shrugged.

"I'm sure he'll think Topher's undeserving of the win he's going to get on Wednesday," she admitted.

"Because he *will* be undeserving." I flexed my fingers, remembering the incredible power I'd felt when I'd controlled Lincoln's sword. "Do you think I'll have to hide my magic forever?"

"I'll make sure you don't," she said. "I know what it feels like to hide your magic—to fear showing people who you truly are. I just need you to hold tight for a bit. Can you do that?"

"I already told you—I won't do to Topher what I did to Lincoln."

"Good," she said. "Now, I think we should head back downstairs. Your fan club awaits."

CHAPTER THIRTEEN

The next morning, we gathered at the soccer field for the face-off between the water champion and the fire champion.

The two people I hated most at the school.

Zane versus Drake—the fire elemental who'd gotten handsy with me at the first party I went to after coming to the academy. Zane had fought him off that night, so it was fitting that he was going to fight him off again.

Since there was a bit of time before the face-off, everyone was mingling near the bleachers. I heard a few bets being made about who people thought would win. It seemed to be a general toss-up between the two.

But I knew better. Zane's immortal strength outweighed Drake's demigod strength by far.

Both of them were standing back with the head teacher of their dorm, getting last-minute tips based on the setup on the field, although Zane didn't appear to be paying much attention. Because he'd caught me looking at him, and he was holding his icy gaze with mine in challenge.

I was telling myself to look away when someone stepped in front of me, blocking my view of Zane.

Vera.

She was wearing all white, and with her long blonde hair flowing down her back in waves, she could have passed for a snow princess. She made a show of looking me up and down, inspecting me, and she frowned, apparently disappointed with what she saw.

"What do you want?" Even though I wanted to walk away from her, I was too curious about whatever she'd come over to say.

"I wanted to see what's so special about you that makes Zane so fascinated with you," she said. "I thought it might be more obvious if I looked closer. But I've still got nothing."

She stared me down like she was waiting for me to come clean.

Did she know about the stupid bond between me and Zane?

"What did he tell you?" I asked.

"Nothing," she said. "He freezes up whenever I mention you."

So, he hadn't filled Vera in on what was going on.

Interesting.

Because that meant he was staying loyal to me. I couldn't help but feel a strange sense of pride about that.

"He's probably embarrassed that I rejected him." I shrugged. "Don't worry—I'm sure he'll get over it eventually."

I almost added that once Zane was over it, Vera could have a go at him again. But I held back. Because given everything Zane had told me the other night about Vera having lost her soulmate, I didn't have the heart to be snarky.

Was it even possible to get over a soulmate bond?

I doubted it.

Which meant I might be pining after a total asshole for the rest of my life.

God help me. Or goddess. Whoever it was that witches and demigods were supposed to pray to.

"You have a secret," Vera observed. "It has something to do with how you beat Lincoln to become the air champion, and how you melted that deadbolt in Zane's door. And whatever it is, it's making Zane obsessed with you."

Obsessed?

That sounded like an overstatement.

It was probably just Vera being jealous that she wasn't getting all his attention anymore.

"I beat Lincoln and melted that deadbolt because I'm good with my magic," I said, which wasn't *totally* a lie. "As for Zane's interest in me, I'm as clueless as you are."

She pursed her lips and frowned. "You're really not interested in him?"

"I want absolutely nothing to do with him."

She held my gaze, then nodded, apparently convinced. "At least you know what's good for you," she said, backing away slightly. "See you around, Summer. And good luck tomorrow against Topher."

She spun around before I could say thanks, then walked over to talk to *Mason* of all people. And from the way he was checking her out, he was definitely interested in whatever she'd gone over there to say.

"What was that about?" a familiar voice asked from behind me.

Jamie. She was holding two steaming cups of coffee, and she offered one to me. She watched me eagerly, like she was anxious about whether I was going to accept the gesture or not.

"Thanks." I took it and had a sip, relieved that it was a latte. I hated the taste of black coffee. "I'm sorry about yesterday," I said, since my friendship with Jamie was more important than anything Vera had to say, and I wanted to address the tension between us first.

"You have nothing to be sorry about," she said simply.

"But you were the one who wanted to compete. I wouldn't have volunteered if it wasn't for you."

"I'm not sure I'd call what happened to you *volunteering*," she said with a warm smile.

"True," I said, since I'd basically been forced.

"But you still won, fair and square," she said. "You deserved that win. And it's not like that was my last chance. I have three more years to up my game and try to be the air dorm champion."

"You're going to be a great champion," I said.

"Oh, I know I will." She raised her cup and drank to that. "Anyway, what's up with Vera?"

My head buzzed with responses that might make sense, since the truth wasn't an option.

Although maybe it sort of was? Not the real truth, but a version of it.

"Vera 'wanted to see what was so special about me' that makes Zane interested." I did my best to imitate her haughty tone.

"So, she's jealous," Jamie said.

"Seems like it."

"Well, she seems to be getting over it quickly." Jamie glanced at where Vera and Mason were chatting. Vera was basically hanging all over him.

"Are students allowed to be involved with teachers?" I asked.

"Technically, no," she said. "But that doesn't mean it doesn't happen."

"Got it," I said, giving Vera and Mason another glance.

Since we had a bit more time before the face-off, Jamie and I chatted more about how epic it was when I took down Lincoln yesterday, and about his expulsion. Eventually, it was time to take our seats to watch Zane and Drake go up against each other. Each dorm had a designated spot on the bleachers, and as the air elemental champion, I sat front and center. Mason sat on one side of me, and Jamie on the other. It was a major change from where I normally would have sat—the back row—but at least I had Jamie by my side again.

Zane and Drake stood at opposite ends of the soccer field, in front of the goal posts. Two lines of weapons were laid out, about twenty feet away from each of them. Swords, daggers, axes, spears, arrows, and more. We'd trained with some of them in our afternoon classes, but there were others I didn't recognize.

Kate made her way to the center of the field, and everyone silenced. She looked around at the bleachers, and when her eyes met mine, it felt like they were cutting into my soul.

I was definitely going to have to grovel at some point to get her to forgive me. Which was unfortunate, because I wasn't one to grovel.

Hopefully she'd cool down on her own.

Or else I was going to have a very angry goddess to deal with.

CHAPTER FOURTEEN

Kate yanked her gaze away from mine and beamed at the crowd.

"Welcome to the first battle round of Greek Week!" she said, and everyone burst into applause. She smiled and patiently waited as the cheering died down. "As is tradition, water will fight fire in the first round, and air will fight earth. A random draw determined that fire and water would face off today. As for the rules—I know most of you know them, but here's a reminder. Each champion has been given a selection of weapons. The winner will be the first one to draw blood using one of the weapons provided."

Last night, the others had explained to me how the rules specifically stated that the first blood had to be drawn with one of the provided weapons. It made it so we needed to use more than just our element to win.

And, ironically, my element was part of nearly every one of those weapons on the field.

"Remember, the battle is until first blood—not to kill," Kate continued, and everyone glanced over at the air section of the bleachers. It hadn't taken long for the entire school to hear about what had happened with me and Lincoln. "If any champion attempts to fatally injure the other, that champion will be expelled immediately." She glanced at Drake, and then at Zane, and they nodded in acknowledgment. Then she walked to the other side of the field and stopped in front of the center bench, where Nicole and Blake were sitting.

Blake stood, counted down, and blew the whistle for them to begin.

Zane and Drake rushed toward their line-up of weapons.

Drake chose a huge wooden ax-like thing with two large blades protruding out of the top.

Zane kept it simple, going for a sleek, silver sword. He swung it around expertly, like he had zero doubts that he was going to win this fight.

Of course he was going to win. Drake had no idea what type of monster he was dealing with.

Not like I felt bad for Drake, given our history.

As expected, Drake didn't hesitate to send a blast of fire at Zane.

Zane moved smoother than water, dancing around the

flames, and sent a group of sharp icicles at Drake. But Drake's fire met them in the middle, melting them as it burned out.

They continued like that for a few minutes—each one trying to attack the other with their element. But fire and water negated each other. It was clearly going to take more than their elements to take the other down.

Drake launched his fire to create a circle of flames around Zane—so high that Zane disappeared inside of it. I held my breath, worried about him, but he quickly put out the fire with ice that melted to water.

Drake released an angry roar, then dropped his ax and picked up a bow and arrow instead. He started launching fiery arrows at Zane, but Zane created a shield of ice with his other hand, easily fending off the arrows.

As he fended them off, he moved closer to Drake, his sword still in hand.

Drake threw down his arrows, held out his hands, and shot a large blast of fire at Zane.

Zane blocked it with his ice shield, although the shield melted into water as the last of the flames died down.

Triumph flashed in Drake's eyes as he prepared to launch more fire.

But in less than a second, Zane launched an icicle through one of Drake's hands, quickly followed by the other.

Drake cried out in agony.

Zane moved in a blur, darting around Drake and using his sword to slice a shallow, clean line across Drake's back. Blood had also managed to get on Drake's lips, so he looked like an angry vampire.

Drake's blood shined in the sunlight, and he stared down at the identical holes in his palms in shock. He didn't move—it was like Zane's ice had frozen him in place.

Blake raised a flare gun, and it let out a loud pop as the flare shot up and exploded into a blue firework above the field.

The students in the water section of the stands stood up and went nuts, cheering and hollering in excitement.

The fire section was quiet, frowning and making low sounds of disappointment.

My section and the earth section clapped as well, although not nearly as enthusiastically as the water students.

"Congratulations, Zane Caldwell!" Kate said. "You've won the first battle round for the water dorm and will proceed to the final competition." She glided over to him, placed an olive wreath on his head, and the water students started cheering again.

Nicole made her way over to Drake, who was now kneeling on the ground, staring at the blood pooling beneath his maimed hands in shock. It hadn't been a lethal injury, but it was still disturbing to see. It was also impossible to look away.

Slowly, she lowered herself down next to him and took his hands in hers. Moments later, she removed her hands, and the holes in his palms were filled.

But Zane was Norse. So how had Nicole healed Drake? She couldn't heal Norse injuries.

Maybe it was different with immortals. After all, Zane *had* told me that the immortals weren't on the side of the Norse gods.

Drake flexed his fists, as if checking to see if they still worked.

Nicole stood up and walked around to his back.

"Leave it," he said, his voice low and intense. "I want to keep it as a souvenir." He glared at Zane, as if silently promising himself that he'd eventually get his revenge.

"Your call." Nicole shrugged and headed back over to Blake and Kate, clearly not caring either way.

The water elementals jumped out of their seats and gathered around Zane, congratulating him and high fiving him. Some of the guys gave him awkward man-hugs, and the girls were beaming at him like they worshipped the ground he walked on.

"I hope you win tomorrow," Jamie said from her seat next to me.

I looked at her in surprise. "You want me to beat Topher?"

"It's not that I want Topher to lose," she said. "I just want you to face off against Zane."

I continued to clap robotically, and, finally, Zane's eyes zeroed in on mine.

Everything he'd told me the other night came flooding back. How he truly believed that the immortals deserved to rule over the Greeks. That he wanted to make everyone here bow down to him and his people. The superior sound in his tone when he'd said it, and how he'd said that I didn't have to worry, because the immortals would protect me.

And as much as I knew I needed to hide my magic and purposefully lose against Topher tomorrow, there was no denying it—I wanted to face off against Zane, too.

CHAPTER FIFTEEN

As I dressed for the face-off against Topher, I kept thinking about the exact promise I'd made to Nicole.

I can't help being in tune with my sword. But I won't use my metal magic on anything else.

Because when I held a sword—or anything made of metal—the weapon felt like it was an extension of me.

Maybe I could beat Topher with my sword fighting skills alone.

Then I'd be able to fight in the final battle against Zane.

Thrills traveled through me again at the thought. But as much as I hated it, I doubted I'd be able to beat Zane without fully using my metal magic against him. And the thought of not putting one hundred percent of my efforts into beating him made me feel sick.

A knock on my door yanked me out of my thoughts.

"Summer?" Jamie poked her head in. "You ready?"

"Yes." I spun around to face her and motioned to my outfit. "How does it look?"

I was wearing the battle uniform provided by the school—a yellow tracksuit lined with wool, so I (hopefully) wouldn't freeze on the field.

I didn't need to look in the mirror to know yellow was a terrible color for me. "Slowly dying of jaundice" wasn't a fashion statement I liked to make. Ever.

"You know it won't kill you to take that sheet off the mirror, right?" Jamie strutted over to the full-length mirror and yanked the sheet off it before I could reply.

Like I already knew, the tracksuit looked terrible on me.

And the skin on my arms prickled with the feeling of being watched.

"Don't you feel that?" I asked her, staying focused on my reflection.

"Feel what?"

"This." I pulled her in front of the mirror, but when I did, the feeling disappeared.

"I don't know what you're talking about," she said slowly, like she was worried I was going insane.

"It's probably just nerves." I shrugged it off, attempting a small smile. "Forget about it."

"Sure." She didn't sound like she believed me, but she

pulled me away from the mirror anyway. "Come on—let's go. You don't want to be late to your own battle round."

Reluctantly, I threw the sheet back over the mirror, and the two of us headed out.

It wasn't long before I was standing on the field with a row of weapons ahead of me and Topher on the other end.

Some of the tips Mason and the others had given me these past two nights floated through my mind. I should pick a sword over any other weapon (obviously), stay light on my feet, and try to win as quickly as possible, since as an earth elemental, Topher could use the environment against me. Depending on how strong he was, something as little as the grass underneath my feet—or even the ground itself—could be a threat.

Topher stared me down, his gaze calculating and deadly. Like he was trying to figure out the exact formula to take me out.

I did my best to look equally intimidating. And I must have succeeded, because he broke eye contact and took a small step back.

It was fun to embrace the whole "dark princess of the Underworld" thing I had going on here.

Kate, Nicole, and Blake sat in their same spot as yesterday—on the center bench that was basically on the field. But this time, they were joined by Zane, who was wearing the wreath of olive branches on his head.

When Zane's gaze met mine, he gave me a small nod, as if to say, *you've got this.*

Really? After I'd bluntly rejected him the other night, he had the nerve to act *supportive?*

The corner of his lips curved up into a small smile, and my cheeks flushed as I looked away, realizing I'd been staring.

Kate stood, and everyone went silent, focusing on her.

"Today, the air champion—Summer—and the earth champion—Topher—will battle in the final playoff round," she said. "The one who draws first blood will continue to the final battle tomorrow and will face off against Zane."

The water dorm cheered at the name of their champion.

If only they knew he didn't have a single drop of Greek blood in him, so he wasn't one of them at all.

I examined the weapons laid out ahead of me and eyed the ones I was going to go for. Energy buzzed off them, like they were ready for me to hold them in my hands.

It would be so easy to hold my hands out and call them into my palms without moving an inch.

But I'd promised Nicole I'd hide my metal magic, and I intended to stick to my word. Which was too bad, because it would be so entertaining to see the expression on Topher's face when those weapons obeyed my command.

Instead, I moved my weight forward onto my toes, ready to sprint forward when the battle began.

Blake counted off, then blew the whistle.

I bolted toward the longsword first.

I was inches away from it, and the handle flew into my palm like a magnet. Hopefully no one noticed, but I didn't have time to look around to check. Anyway, it could probably pass as regular air magic.

Hopefully.

I pivoted toward the other side of the line-up, ready to grab the shiny, sharp dagger waiting for me there.

My hand got stuck in a wall of grass on its way there.

The grass had *grown* between my hand and the dagger, and the blades were crawling around my fingers, trying to trap me. They slithered over my skin like tiny worms, and disgust recoiled through me.

Topher ran at me.

As he got closer, the grass tightened its hold on me. I was stuck. My hand tingled, losing circulation.

Get off *me*, I thought to the grass, giving my hand a small shake.

It loosened enough for me to squirm out of it and run to the side.

Topher fell through the empty space where I'd been

standing. His eyes widened in surprise, and he stumbled, but he recovered quickly.

I ran at him and launched myself into the air, my sword raised overhead.

He raised his sword, and it clashed against mine.

I could *so* easily knock his sword out of his hands with my magic. Send it flying across the field. Use his surprise to my advantage and slice his arm, ending this fight before it had a chance to really begin.

Instead, I let him fight fair. Well, fair-ish. Because I allowed him full control of his sword. Still, I was naturally in tune with his weapon enough to match him swing for swing and blow for blow. My actual footing and movements were terrible, but I was able to stop his blade from cutting my skin.

"You've gotten pretty good at this for someone who's only been here for a month." He wasn't even the slightest bit out of breath when he spoke.

I "answered" by perfectly blocking his next blow.

He scowled, spun around, and ran about fifteen feet away. As I was running toward him to take another strike, he kneeled and dug his fingers into the ground.

Something tugged at my ankles, stopping me midstride.

I somehow managed to stop myself from falling flat on my face, and I glanced down to see what was trapping me.

Grass.

Topher had *made the grass grow* and used it to create "grass handcuffs" around my ankles.

This battlefield was literally made of his element. He had an incredible amount of control here, and from the arrogant expression on his face, he knew it.

In this situation, an air elemental could create a cushion of air between their feet and the ground, float themselves up a few inches, then use their sword to cut the grass, freeing themselves.

That clearly wasn't an option for me.

I could technically use my sword to cut the grass off my ankles. But the grass was wound tight, so I'd have to allow the blade to cut my skin. Anything else would be too suspicious. And I didn't particularly want to mutilate myself, since it would weaken me.

I didn't want to lower myself to losing against Topher because I'd injured myself with my own element.

So, I tugged one foot up as hard as possible to try to rip the grass from the ground.

I got it in one try.

Victory.

Topher's eyes widened in surprise.

He clearly hadn't expected the new kid to be so good.

Because I *shouldn't* be so good.

I also hated losing. But I had to do it. Maybe it was best to get it over with before I could talk myself out of it.

I itched to tug out my other foot as well. But then I'd quickly free myself and be able to sword fight him again. And everyone had already seen that I was more than capable with a sword.

To make this believable, I needed to look weakened.

Which meant keeping my ankle trapped.

I made a show of trying to pull it up, but I didn't use nearly as much force as I had with the other foot. The grass felt ready to snap, and if I kept pulling up, I knew I'd break free. It would be so easy. The temptation swirled inside me, inviting me to unleash more of my magic and show the entire school what I was made of.

Instead, I stared at the grass wrapped around my ankle and narrowed my eyes in frustration.

The audience collectively held their breath.

Topher ran at me, sword in hand, ready to strike.

I held my sword up to guard myself, protecting myself against his first blow as it crashed down on my sword.

He pushed his blade against mine and scowled, as if my mere existence enraged him.

I wanted to slice that smile off his face.

Instead, I leaned back and grunted to make it look like my strength was waning.

"You shouldn't have been able to do that," he growled, and then he pulled back and hurried around to stand behind me.

With my ankle tied to the ground, I couldn't rotate

myself enough to fight him. But if I broke free now, I could protect myself against his next blow, catch him off-guard, and win this thing.

If I won, I'd fight against Zane tomorrow.

At the thought of Zane, I glanced at where he was sitting on the center bench with Nicole, Blake, and Kate. His gaze was intense, and I couldn't tell if he wanted me to win so we could face off in the final battle round, or if he wanted me to lose so he wouldn't have to fight me.

None of it mattered, because Topher swiped his sword against the back of my arm.

As the sharp end of the blade traced over my skin, I told my body to allow it to break through.

My skin broke apart. Heat seared through me, followed by the wet feeling of blood.

I gasped and stared down at the cut on my arm. It was only a few inches long—no serious damage done.

At least Topher hadn't lost it like Lincoln. But from the angry way he was still looking at me, I could have sworn he wanted to.

Chills crept over me at the thought.

What did Topher mean when he said I "shouldn't have been able to do that?" I shouldn't have been able to break free of his grass trap?

Probably not with brute force. That had to be the sort of thing one expected from a trained demigod.

Maybe he was catching on to the fact that I was a demigod and not a witch gifted with elemental magic.

A firework explosion overhead yanked me out of my thoughts. A *green* firework.

"Congratulations, Topher!" Kate said. "You've won your battle round and will compete against Zane in the final showdown tomorrow."

My eyes met Nicole's, and she nodded in satisfaction.

Shame rushed through me. Because I'd just gone against every gut instinct of mine and *let* someone win.

It wasn't right. I stared down at the sword I was still holding, feeling like I'd failed it.

The earth elementals rushed around Topher to congratulate him, huge smiles on their faces. Kate placed the wreath on his head, crowning him the winner.

The entire time, Topher's sharp eyes remained locked on mine. Unlike the others, he wasn't smiling.

He knew something.

And as much as I wished otherwise, I had a feeling he wasn't going to forget this until he uncovered every last one of my secrets.

CHAPTER SIXTEEN

That night, I locked myself in my room. Jamie knocked on my door to try to talk, and she thankfully seemed understanding when I told her I needed time to myself.

Kate sent me a simple text telling me she was happy to see that I did my best.

The innuendo was clear—I'd done my best at *trying* to fail.

Nicole had also sent me a text to check in, and I'd told her I needed some space.

Not that it was doing me much good. My mind was spinning too much to get lost in the book I'd been reading, but I was able to find a television show to veg out on. I nearly finished an entire season before passing out for the night.

I woke to someone pounding on my door and screaming my name.

Jamie.

My brain felt foggy, but somehow, I dragged myself out of bed and opened the door.

Her eyes widened in horror at the sight of my assumably disastrous state. "Zane and Topher face off in thirty minutes," she said. "Please tell me you weren't still sleeping?"

"Guilty," I muttered, shocked at myself for having slept for so long.

The fight against Topher yesterday must have taken more out of me than I'd realized. Like I'd flexed a muscle I wasn't accustomed to using.

The muscle of *losing a competition on purpose.*

"Hurry up and get dressed," she said. "You're expected to sit in the front row looking your best and cheering them on. Anything else would show bad sportsmanship."

"Is it bad sportsmanship that I'm not rooting for either one of them?" I asked.

"Come on." She rolled her eyes. "We both know you're rooting for Zane."

I froze at the thought of rooting for someone who was literally here to figure out a way for his race to overpower everyone at this school. No one here should root for him.

They should expel him the same way they'd done to Lincoln.

Except if they knew Zane's secret, they wouldn't simply *expel* him.

They'd kill him.

My heart twisted with pain, just like it always did when I thought about any harm coming to Zane. Like the thought of him being in pain hurt me, too.

"He really did a number on you, didn't he?" Jamie asked.

"You have no idea," I said, and then I rushed to get ready and hurried with Jamie to the field.

As the champion of my element, I sat in the front row of the bleachers for the air students. It was much chillier today than it had been all week, and I wrapped my arms around myself, trying not to shiver.

Mason sauntered up and stood in front of me. His shadow blocked me from the sunlight, like he thought he was some sort of god. He had the same arrogant smirk on his face as always, and appeared totally unaffected by the cold.

I braced myself for him to ram into me for my loss against Topher.

"That was a solid showing yesterday," he said instead,

and I tilted my head in confusion, waiting for a snide comment about how I should be on the field right now instead of Topher.

Which, admittedly, I should have been.

"The way you escaped the grass he wound around your ankles was... unique, to say the least," he continued.

"Wow." I lifted my chin and sat back in surprise. "Was that a *compliment?*"

"Just curiosity," he said. "It wasn't the move I expected for someone in your position."

No kidding.

"I just tugged really hard." I shrugged. "No big deal."

He eyed me suspiciously, like he was expecting me to elaborate.

I didn't. I refused to be broken by something as simple as an intimidating gaze.

His smirk grew, like he was amused by my non-response. "You're stronger than you realize," he finally said. "Which *is* a big deal, even if you say it isn't."

With that, he plopped down in the space next to me.

Jamie waggled her eyebrows and sat at my other side.

Nicole, Blake, and Kate were standing at their same place on the field-side bench. Kate gave me a short nod of acknowledgment about what I'd done yesterday. Nicole and Blake were deep in conversation about something else.

Zane and Topher stood at opposing sides of the field.

It was nearly the exact same setup as the past two days, minus the fact that the rows of weapons were closer to the center, to force them into tighter fighting grounds.

Kate looked at our side of the bleachers, and then at the opposing side, where the water and fire students sat.

Everyone quieted.

"Welcome to the final battle of Greek Week," she said, and everyone burst into applause. Most of the excitement came from the earth and water sections, which was unsurprising, given that their champions were the ones facing off today. "As you know, today the winners from the first two battle rounds will face off. Zane and Topher have demonstrated incredible skill and power over their magic to get to this point. And soon, we'll crown our king of this year's Greek Week."

It should have been a queen, I thought.

But even if I was standing in Topher's place right now, Zane would still probably win. Unless he was trying to hide the extent of his magic like I was, although judging from his first battle round, that didn't appear to be the case.

I glanced at the water bleachers and found Vera sitting alone in the back corner, her expression cold. She was the only one in her section who wasn't excited.

Maybe she was like Kate and the others, and didn't want Zane to show his full strength. She had to be worried about their secret getting out.

You have a secret, her words from the other day replayed in my mind.

As if she were one to talk.

"Earth to Summer." Jamie nudged me. "You okay?"

"Yeah." I pasted on a fake smile. "Of course."

She didn't look like she believed me.

But it didn't matter, because Blake stood up and blew the whistle for the fight to begin.

Zane and Topher rushed forward.

Like before, Zane went for the longsword. He always looked so fierce and deadly with a longsword. It was like the weapon was made for him.

Topher went for a spiked ball on a chain. It looked brutally dangerous, like it could take down Zane's sword in one swing.

Zane just raised an eyebrow and gave Topher a look like he was daring him to come at him.

Topher swung his weapon around and smiled arrogantly, as if he thought he had this one in the bag, and rushed toward Zane.

Zane simply stood there, hand outstretched, and shot a blast of ice at Topher's weapon. The ice covered the ball and chain, freezing it midair like it was a statue. The chain remained in the same curved shape it had been in while Topher had been swinging it.

Topher's mouth widened in shock, and he dropped

the weapon to the ground. The ice stayed frozen, the chain not budging.

Everyone in the bleachers gasped.

Vera huffed and rolled her eyes, seemingly the only one unimpressed.

Topher rushed to grab another weapon, but he was too late. Because Zane flashed to him in a blur and swiped the tip of his sword down Topher's arm in what I imagined must have been the quickest final battle-round win in the school's history.

The students in the earth section groaned and muttered in disappointment.

Topher's blood dripped down onto the grass as he stood there, shocked. Like Drake, he also had blood on his lips. His eyes went back and forth between glaring at Zane and the frozen ball and chain on the ground.

The students in the water section stood, clapping and hollering in excitement. I couldn't see Vera anywhere. She'd either left or remained seated.

Blake shot blue fireworks into the air, and they exploded overhead in a succession of pops and bangs.

"Congratulations, Zane Caldwell!" Kate beamed, clearly pleased with the outcome of the fight. "The official winner of this year's Greek Week!"

The water section cheered louder and rushed over to congratulate him. Vera was still sitting on the bench, scowling.

Nicole walked toward Topher and healed the slash on his arm. Topher's eyes remained frozen—dead. Like he was lost in his own thoughts. Nicole said something to him, and he walked with her over to the main bench with Blake and Kate.

"Summer and Drake, please join us at the winner's bench," Kate said.

I glared at Drake, not wanting to be anywhere near him.

Jamie nudged me again. "Go to the bench," she said, and I stood robotically and did as asked, refusing to look at Zane, Drake, or Topher as I approached Nicole's side.

I just had to get through this, then I could go back to my room and zone out on TV for the rest of the night.

Kate reached into a box next to the bench and pulled out a wreath made of gold branches and leaves. As she did, the water students moved away from Zane to give him space.

Kate locked her eyes with his and said, "Please come forward and accept your crown."

Zane did as asked, although his eyes were fixed on mine the entire time.

I couldn't look away, no matter how much I wished I could. It was like he'd trapped me in his gaze, and I was frozen in place just as much as the ball and chain that Topher had tried to use against him.

Kate held the wreath toward him. "Please kneel," she instructed.

Zane lowered himself onto one knee, although he didn't face Kate—he faced me.

I sucked in a sharp breath of icy air.

Why was he looking at me like he was about to make a marriage proposal?

"Summer Donovan," he said my name slowly, with a knowing glint in his eyes. "Will you do me the honor of being my date to the ball tomorrow night?"

The crowd hushed. My vocal cords suddenly felt just as frozen as the rest of me, but I swallowed and got a hold of myself.

"Are you kidding me?" I said the first thing that popped into my mind.

"I can assure you that I am one hundred percent not kidding you." He stared up at me in earnest. "As the King of Greek Week, the ball tomorrow night will be held in my honor. It would be my ultimate pleasure to have you by my side throughout the entirety of it."

He sounded different than ever before. So confident and poised.

He was speaking like he was a king.

That was what he thought he was, wasn't it? Not just the King of Greek Week—he thought the immortals were the rulers of the world. And just like he'd said to me at the lake, he wanted me by his side as they ruled.

If this was some sort of test or promise of what was to come, I wanted nothing to do with it.

"No," I said, and he flinched, his eyes twisting with pain as if I'd physically hurt him. "I'm going by myself."

His expression flattened. It was the same ambivalent way he'd looked at me when he'd lied and said he didn't remember the first night we'd spent together, and seeing him shut down like that hurt me deep in my soul. "Very well," he said, and then, as if nothing had happened, he turned to Kate and accepted his crown.

I glanced back over at the bleachers where the water students had been sitting to see Vera's reaction, but she was already gone.

Then, as if she knew I was thinking about her, my watch buzzed with a text.

From Vera.

We need to talk. 3 AM tonight. My room—the one at the very top of the water tower. Don't tell Zane.

It was quickly followed by another message.

Your watch will be able to unlock the door to the water dorm. So don't worry about how you're getting in.

Another typing bubble, and she added, *I'll see you soon.*

Nothing more after that.

I stared at the texts in shock. Because what on Earth was that about? Was she angry with me about embarrassing Zane? Had Zane told her the truth about me? About *us?*

He was unpredictable enough that it wouldn't surprise me if he had.

More importantly—would she hurt me because of it? She was an immortal, after all. I knew better than to underestimate her.

But if she tried anything, someone would know, since we'd be in the dorm. She wouldn't be stupid enough to do something like that.

I didn't immediately reply. But I knew without question that I'd go. Because despite how much I disliked Vera, I was far too curious to do anything else.

CHAPTER SEVENTEEN

The air students were too busy during dinner, chatting about who they were going with to the ball, to bother hounding me with questions. I'd lost the competition, which meant I was old news by now.

Thank God.

Once I was back in my room, time moved at a snail's pace as I waited for 3 AM. I didn't get any more texts from Vera, and I still hadn't replied to hers. She knew I'd be there.

I'd always thought of 3 AM as the "witching hour"—late enough that even night owls were sleeping, but early enough that the early birds had yet to rise. As expected, when I left the dorm, I didn't pass anyone in the halls. And as I walked to the water dorm, no one was outside.

It was also *freezing*. A glance at my watch showed it was almost zero degrees Fahrenheit. Everything was so quiet and still that it was like the freezing air had stopped time itself.

I approached the water dorm and walked up the stairs to the door. My watch was only supposed to be able to unlock the door to the air dorm, and to my room.

But when I held it up to the scanner, the lock clicked open.

I stared at my watch in shock.

How did Vera know it would be able to do that? Had she somehow *made* it do that? Did immortals have some sort of power over technology that Zane hadn't mentioned to me?

I had *so many questions.*

I pulled the door open, bracing myself for someone to be in the common room and demand to know what I was doing there. I had no idea what I'd say if that happened. I probably should have planned for it, just in case.

But like everywhere else on campus, the main floor of the water dorm was empty.

I hurried up the circular steps to the top of the water tower, doing my best to be as quiet as possible. There were only two doors at the top of the building—one for Vera, and the other for her suitemate. But she hadn't told me which door was which.

Not wanting to accidentally wake her suitemate, I took out my phone and texted her that I was there.

The door closer to me swung open. Vera. She wore a

short, white, flowing dress, and her long hair fell in perfect blonde waves down her back.

No one should have the right to look that perfectly beautiful at three in the morning.

She looked me up and down in approval, even though I was sure I looked a mess in my layers of winter gear, messy hair, and cheeks burnt red from the cold. She wasn't scowling or smirking, which made this the friendliest she'd ever looked in my presence.

"Come in," she said, stepping aside for me to enter.

"Thanks." I cleared my throat, unsure what else to say, and walked into her room.

It was pristinely neat, decorated in all whites and grays. Like Zane, she had metal prints of glaciers and mountains hanging on her walls. There were no pops of color *anywhere.*

And her mirror was turned to face the wall.

"You feel it, too?" I asked after she'd closed the door.

"The sense of someone watching me?" she asked.

"Yes."

"I don't," she said, and disappointment filled me. "But Zane told me you did, and I figured it was best to be safe."

"So you don't know who's watching?"

"You seem to be the only one who can feel it." She waited, as if she expected me to explain why.

"I don't know any more about the mirrors than you

do," I said softly, glancing at the door to the bathroom hall that connected the room to her suitemate's.

"Don't worry about anyone hearing us," she said. "I don't have a suitemate. I don't like sharing."

Her voice took on a sharp edge at that last part.

"Are you talking about Zane?" I asked. "Because I already told you—I'm not interested."

"You made that more than clear when you rejected him in front of the entire school today," she said. "Although I don't understand why you did it. You know that rejecting a soulmate bond is futile, right?"

"He told you," I said, unsurprised after the mysteriousness of her texts.

"He did." Her eyes were sharp and hard.

Deadly.

Immortal.

I backed toward the door, my stomach twisting with nerves.

I shouldn't have come.

Maybe I'd been naïve in thinking she wouldn't bring me here to hurt me. From her icy stare, I had a feeling she wouldn't hesitate if killing me was her goal.

I reached out with my mind to feel for any metal in the room, ready to use it to defend myself. The metal prints on the walls were particularly interesting. Sharp ends on all sides that could make them fantastic flying weapons.

"Relax," she said. "I'm not going to hurt you. You're one of us now."

"I'm *not* one of you," I said. "I'm not a—"

"A monster?" she challenged.

I held her gaze, unwilling to back down. "He told you I called him that."

"He did," she said. "And you're not wrong. The Norse gods see us as monsters as well. But it's only because they're intimidated by us. They know we're meant to rule, and they're scared of the day when it will finally happen again."

I huffed in annoyance at the lecture about the immortals being the "superior" supernatural race. I'd gotten enough of it from Zane. I didn't need it from her, too.

She motioned to her sofa. "Would you like to have a seat?"

"No," I said instinctively. "I'd rather stand."

"Your choice." She shrugged, but remained standing as well.

The tension between us was thick, and I remained ready to slice it with one of those metallic prints if necessary.

"Why did you ask me to come here?" I asked, since if she was going to hurt me, she probably would have done it by now.

"We need to talk about the remaining handmaiden," she said. "Fulla."

I tilted my head in surprise. "What about her?"

"She's being held captive in the academy for questioning. It won't be long for her to break and tells them our secret."

"It's not *our* secret," I said. "It's *yours.*"

She raised a perfectly plucked eyebrow. "Zane's your soulmate," she said simply. "His secret is your secret. Which therefore makes it *our* secret."

I wanted to tell her she was wrong.

But we both knew it would be a lie. And dancing around the truth was the last thing I felt like doing. I'd been doing so much of it that simply the thought of it exhausted me.

"If you were going to tell anyone, you would have by now," she continued confidently, staring at me in challenge. "But you won't do anything to hurt your soulmate like that. You physically *can't.*"

The pain I felt whenever I thought about anyone hurting Zane. She'd felt it, too. With her soulmate.

"Maybe not," I said, since there was no point in denying it. "But I won't do anything to hurt the others at the school, either."

"Helping us kill Fulla won't hurt the others at the school."

I flinched back, stunned. "Wait… what?"

"Killing Fulla," she repeated slowly, like she was

talking to an idiot. "Shutting her up before she spills what she knows."

"You can't just break into her prison and kill her," I sputtered.

"Why not?"

It was a good question. Especially since I had no idea what immortals were truly capable of doing.

"Because if you could, you'd have done it already," I said.

"You're right—if we could do it alone, we'd have done it already," she said. "But we can't. We need your help."

Vera was up to something. I just needed to figure out what that something was.

To do that, I needed to keep her talking.

"Why would powerful immortals need my help for anything?" I asked.

"Because of your magic," she said. "The one over metal. The one you used to melt the bolt in Zane's door and lock us inside his room."

"Nothing that a powerful fire elemental can't do." I shrugged it off like it was easy.

"But we don't have a powerful fire elemental on our side," she said. "We have you. So, we're going to have to learn how to work together, and quickly."

"I'm not on your side," I fired back.

"Oh, you are." She smiled, as if she was confident I was lying.

"I take it you have a plan?" I finally asked.

"Does that mean you're in?"

"It means I want to know the plan."

She appraised me, the corner of her lips turning up into a knowing smirk. "I do have a plan," she said. "But if I tell you and you don't help, then I'll have to kill you, too."

CHAPTER EIGHTEEN

Another wave of panic rushed through me.

"I'm joking." She chuckled. "Even if you know our plan, I know you won't tell anyone. I didn't bring you here to hurt you."

"You're putting a lot of trust in me," I said.

"Like I said, I know what it's like to have a soulmate," she said. "I know the lengths you'll go to make sure he remains safe. So, you might as well drop the pretense that you're not on our side, and learn how you're going to help us."

"There's no pretense here." I glanced around her cold, sterile room, then refocused on her. "There's also one big thing that isn't right."

"And what's that?"

"Zane. You keep saying that you understand the soulmate bond, how I'll never hurt my soulmate, and all that stuff. So why are you the one telling me all this? Why not have him here, too?"

"Firstly, because after you turned Zane down when he invited you to the ball, it would have brought a *lot* of attention to both of you if anyone saw you together," she said. "It doesn't hurt to be overly cautious when it comes to these things."

"Of course," I said, as if plotting to break into the secret on-campus prison to kill the goddess being kept captive there was something I did on a regular basis.

"Secondly," she continued. "Zane's busy right now."

"Busy doing what?"

"He's in the main kitchen," she said. "Adding a special ingredient to the champagne we'll be drinking for the toast at the ball tomorrow night. Well, the champagne *they'll* be drinking. You won't be partaking in the celebratory sip."

I didn't know what I'd expected her to say, but that certainly hadn't been it.

"How did he get into the kitchen?" I asked what was probably far from the highest priority question here.

"How did you get into the water dorm?" she answered my question with one of her own.

"Good question." I stood strongly in place, not wanting Vera to think she intimidated me—even though she most definitely did. "One I've been wondering myself."

"Ever since being released from the ice, I've found I have quite the knack with modern-day technology," she said. "It's why I was chosen to join Zane in infiltrating the school."

At least she wasn't trying to spin what they were doing into anything other than the fact that they were spying.

"So, you hacked into the watches," I said.

"I hacked the *system*," she corrected me. "It took about a year and a half to figure it out, but since then, it's felt like child's play. I quite enjoy using my gift."

"You make it sound like magic."

"Because it is," she said. "Some of us have unique gifts, and I'm one of them."

"And Zane?" I asked.

"He hasn't told you his yet?"

"Would I be asking if he had?"

"Good point," she said, and I readied myself for anything. "But that's something he should share with you—not me."

Seriously?

"I guess that's fair," I said, since when she put it that way, it was. "Is he a gifted poisoner or something?"

"Definitely not." She chuckled, as if the idea was ridiculous. "His gift has nothing to do with what he's doing to the champagne right now."

"Adding a special ingredient," I repeated what she'd said earlier.

"Correct."

"What type of ingredient?"

"Immortal mead," she said in a sing-song way, like she'd intended for me to ask—like she'd intended for this conversation to go by a script I'd been unknowingly following.

"And what's that?" I asked cautiously.

"Exactly what it sounds like," she said. "Mead—a honey wine—drank by immortals and Norse gods. When we drink it, it affects us like alcohol affects humans. When anyone non-Norse drinks it... well, let's just say they won't remember much of the ball."

I narrowed my eyes in suspicion. "Will it hurt them?"

"Not any more than over-drinking and blacking out will hurt a human," she said.

"And why should I trust you?"

"You don't have much of a reason to." She shrugged. "But do you trust Zane?"

"He wants to take power away from the Greeks *and* the Norse gods so the immortals can rule the universe," I said. "So, in this instance, no, I don't trust him."

She eyed me like I was prey she could stomp on at any moment. "What exactly do you think the mead will do?" she asked. "Kill them? Because it won't. We don't want to kill anyone here. Well, except for Fulla. The mead will just make it so no one will have any idea that the three of us left the ball. They'll have been too wasted to remember anything."

"And how do you know that everyone will drink it?" I asked.

"This is the third Greek Week ball I'll have attended," she said. "Everyone participates in at least the first sip. It'll be enough for the mead to do what it needs to do."

"Fine," I said, since as much as I hated it, I was starting to believe her. "But don't you think they'll notice that the champagne's been tampered with?"

"Not with the technique Zane's using," she said. "It's called tradecraft. It's easy—you can look it up online later if you want to learn how it's done."

"I doubt it's easy," I said.

"It is for us," she said smugly.

I wanted to smack that smug smile off her perfect face.

But I restrained myself. Because if I wanted to learn this plan of theirs, violence wasn't going to get me anywhere. Except for possibly killed. Which clearly wasn't in *my* plan.

"And where do I come into play?" I asked, surprising myself by how calm I sounded.

"I'm glad you asked," she said, and then she explained what she and Zane had planned for the ball tomorrow night, and what they wanted me to do to help.

CHAPTER NINETEEN

"Which one do you think?" Jamie asked me after coming into my room to get my opinion on which of two dresses she should wear to the ball.

She wore a long blue gown, and was holding a short yellow dress on a hanger. She kept waffling between them, but given that there were only ten minutes until we had to leave, it was time for her to make a choice.

It hadn't been a difficult choice for me, since a black dress was always my go-to in these sorts of situations. Not like I'd ever gone to an actual ball—let alone one I was planning on sneaking out of to help immortals kill a god—so my dress was far from my most important concern.

"I like the one you have on," I said. "You look like a princess."

"But do you think the yellow one might be more eye-catching?"

I studied it closer and gave it some thought. I'd been going over the plan for tonight so many times that anxiety had overrun my brain hours ago, so it was nice to have something else to focus on for a minute.

"It'll pop against your skin," I decided.

"So that's a yes?"

"Yeah," I said. "But I'm not the one to trust for fashion advice."

My gaze naturally went to the door that led to Alyssa's room. Jamie's did, too. Nicole had told me earlier that Alyssa was stable, but her condition hadn't changed. And my mom still wasn't answering my texts. I'd lit a candle earlier to pray for Alyssa's health, but it felt like far from enough.

And who was I to play the martyr, when I'd somehow found myself on the side of the villains?

"You have a better eye than you think." Jamie appraised my outfit again. "Are you sure you don't want to wear heels with that?"

"I hate heels," I said, since it was the truth. "Especially while dancing."

And especially when planning on leaving a ball to help kill a goddess.

This was insane.

Why was I doing this?

Because Zane and Vera are right, I thought the same thing that had been haunting me all day. *The longer Fulla's there, the more likely it is that she'll break and reveal their secret. And if that happens...*

My heart hurt again at the possibilities of what they might do to Zane.

Besides, Fulla was an enemy of the Greeks, too. She'd come to the school to kill us. Killing her would be no different than killing the handmaiden who'd attacked me and Zane in the forest.

But none of it changed the fact that I was about to betray Kate, Nicole, Blake, and everyone else here who had helped me.

Although I was already going behind their backs by keeping Zane's secret.

There was only so much longer I could go before picking a side.

I wished there was someone I could talk to about this. But my mom was far from who I thought she was, my best friend was unaware of the supernatural world, and my suitemate was in a coma.

I was alone.

The only people who knew everything I was dealing with were Zane and Vera. Which was an insanely terrifying thought.

"Topher's waiting downstairs," Jamie said while texting on her phone. "Are you sure you don't want to go with Greg? He still doesn't have a date."

"I'm sure," I said, and we walked down the stairs to

the first floor, where people had gathered to meet up with their dates.

Topher waited at the bottom of the stairs with Greg and Mason. They all wore jackets and ties, and while Topher and Greg looked handsome, Mason looked agitated and uncomfortable. Like the tie was a noose he was dying to rip off his neck.

He watched my every move with cat-like precision, his hair tied back in its normal man-bun, like he was ready to go into fighting-mode at any second.

Beneath the suits and dresses, we all were. Because magic ran in our blood, ready to be called on no matter what we were wearing or what we were doing.

Greg stared at me with wide, puppy-dog eyes as I made my final descent down the stairs.

"You look beautiful," he said.

"Thanks." I smiled uneasily, hoping the neutral acceptance of his compliment would be enough to stop him from getting any ideas.

"Are you sure you don't want a date to the ball tonight?"

No such luck.

"I'm sure," I said in what I hoped was a firm-but-polite tone. "Like I said on the field yesterday, I'm going by myself."

"Whatever you want." He shrugged, spun around, and left the room.

"He'll get over it," Jamie said quickly.

Topher smiled smugly. "He's used to being second best."

For a quiet guy who didn't like to party, Topher was turning out to be way more sly than he'd originally appeared. There was something mysterious, dark, and alluring about him—it was probably why Jamie kept going back to him.

She didn't like anything that came easy. Especially when it came to men.

Mason smirked as he watched Greg walk away, then turned his mischievous gaze back to mine. "I believe this is the first time in the academy's history that a champion of their element has gone to the ball without a date," he said.

"Setting records seems to be my specialty around here," I said grimly.

"You say that like it's a bad thing."

"It hasn't been the greatest."

He raised an eyebrow, like he'd just gotten an idea. "Then let me help you out by escorting you to the ball."

"Really?" I balked. "You're my teacher."

I remembered what Jamie had told me about some teachers secretly hooking up with students, but I didn't think a teacher would ever be so *blatant* with their attempts.

"I'm not asking you to be my date," he said, as if my comment was ridiculous.

"Then what are you asking?"

"I'm asking to escort you." He straightened, suddenly looking more at ease than ever in his suit. "I'm the leader of the air elemental dorm. Escorting my champion to the ball would be my honor."

"I don't see how being 'escorted' to the ball with my teacher would draw less attention than going alone," I said.

"It might not." He shrugged, that mischievous glint still in his eyes. "But it would certainly be unexpected, especially given how blatantly you turned down Zane on the field. As I like to say—if you're going to surprise someone, why not do it with some style?"

He winked, and I rolled my eyes. Because while he was charming in a swoon-worthy romance novel hero sort of way, the last thing I needed was to launch *another* surprise on everyone.

"I'm good with going by myself," I said, and he frowned, apparently caught off-guard by my rejection. "But thanks for the offer."

He quickly regained control of himself. "Anytime," he said smoothly.

I nodded, glad he hadn't insisted, then turned my focus to Jamie.

She was wide-eyed, shocked.

Topher was studying Mason like he was trying—and failing—to figure him out.

I guessed it wouldn't be as normal for a teacher to "escort" a student to the ball as Mason had claimed.

"Are you guys ready?" I asked them, brushing off my unease so Mason wouldn't realize how uncomfortable I felt about his proposition.

I had enough on my plate. I refused to allow him—or anyone—to have power over me like that.

"Ready as ever." Jamie smiled and reached for Topher's hand. "We need to make sure we get good seats."

I nodded politely at Mason, whose gaze had hardened so much that it was impossible to read, then left the dorm with Jamie and Topher to head to the ball.

CHAPTER TWENTY

The gym looked *nothing* like the basketball court I'd become accustomed to training in.

It had been transformed into a winter wonderland in celebration of Zane being King of Greek Week. The dance floor looked like an iced-over lake, and the banquet tables surrounding it displayed various ice sculptures of the Greek gods. At the DJ booth in the back, one of the descendants of Apollo oversaw the music, trying to rile up the crowd as if he was performing at a club in Miami instead of a school dance.

Nicole, Blake, and Kate stood in front of the center of the banquet table in the back, right where we walked in, which was clearly where they'd be sitting during dinner.

"Welcome," Kate said warmly. "And congratulations again to the two of you for your excellent showings on the field this week."

Topher scoffed, and I didn't blame him. His showing against Zane was hardly "excellent."

There was also a serious undertone to Kate's voice—like she was proud of me for deciding my own self-preservation was more important than proving my strength to the entire school. Which was good, since as tough as it was to purposefully lose, I was proud of myself for resisting the temptation of my magic, too.

"Want to sit with me?" Nicole motioned to the seat next to her. "This one's open."

My eyes instantly went to the empty champagne glasses at each place setting, and a lump of guilt and anxiety formed in my throat.

How was I supposed to sit with her and pretend like everything was normal given what was poised to happen tonight?

"I promised Penny and some of the others that I'd sit with them," I lied. "Sorry."

"Oh." She frowned in disappointment—and hurt. "Okay. No problem."

Jamie looked at me with question, but didn't say anything.

I didn't know why I'd specifically named Penny. I could have been more generic in my lie. I could have just said I'd promised some of the other air students I'd sit with them. Nicole wouldn't have known any differently. Now I needed to message Penny to make sure we'd sit together—which I didn't imagine would be a problem, given how we'd bonded after both fighting Lincoln.

But I needed to take this as a lesson for the future. Whenever I needed to lie, it was best to be as unspecific as possible. Fewer details would leave fewer webs to get tangled in.

"Speaking of, we should make sure to save enough seats." Jamie pulled me away, and we hurried to an empty section of the banquet table.

I happily followed her lead.

"What was that about?" she asked when we were out of their ear shots.

"What was what about?" I tried to act clueless.

"I don't remember you promising Penny that you'd sit with her."

"I didn't." I swallowed and tried to come up with a lie—quickly. "I just thought it would be best to sit with other air students, since I was the air elemental champion and all. But I didn't want to make Nicole feel bad, and that was what came out of my mouth first." I shrugged and forced a small smile, as if it was an honest mistake.

Topher's eyes narrowed. "You're terrible at lying," he said. "Has anyone ever told you that?"

My heart stopped.

He knew I was lying to them. But how else could I explain away the lie I'd told them about why I didn't want to sit with Nicole?

This was a mess. I wasn't going to last much longer keeping all these secrets. The pressure in my chest was already building so much that I felt like I was going to explode.

"But I think Nicole believed you," he continued, and I relaxed at the realization that he thought I was lying to *Nicole*, and not to him and Jamie.

Maybe I wasn't as bad at lying as he thought.

"No worries!" Jamie said brightly. "I just texted Penny that we were saving seats for her. She said thanks. All is good."

"Cool," I said, relieved that was done with.

After all, I had so much more to worry about tonight than something stupid like lying about who I was sitting with.

"Now, I don't know about you guys, but I'm *hungry*," she said. "The food's always amazing at the ball, so I've barely eaten all day. Let's go check out the appetizers?"

"Sounds good," I said, and I avoided looking at Nicole the entire way to the buffet.

Students kept trickling into the gym, until nearly all the seats at the tables were taken.

I wasn't hungry, but I forced myself to eat some of the

appetizers. I needed food in my system for what was going to happen next.

Eventually the music stopped, and Kate glided across the dance floor with a glass of champagne in hand, stopping in front of the DJ booth. As we quieted, some of the older witches entered with bottles of champagne and started pouring it into the glasses at all our place settings. Sure, we weren't all twenty-one, but this was a school full of witches and demigods. Human rules didn't apply on school grounds.

Standing there watching us, Kate looked like a queen in her own right—especially in her emerald gown. "It's time to welcome the champion of Greek Week and his date for this evening," she said. "Everyone, please return to your seats for the celebratory toast."

My feet felt heavy, like they were chained to the ground, but I made it over to my seat anyway.

Jamie sat next to me, and Penny across. Mason had somehow managed to claim the seat on my other side. I gave him a polite nod, then focused on the champagne in front of me.

I was far from an expert, but the champagne looked so *normal*. And from the casual way everyone else reached for their glasses, they had no idea anything was amiss.

"All four of our champions this week fought well," Kate said. "And it's my pleasure to present the guest of honor—the winner of this year's Greek Week—Zane Caldwell!"

At her cue, Zane entered from one of the back doors, with Vera at his side.

His suit, shirt, and tie were all black, making him look like a beautiful, deadly creature of the night. How no one else realized he was so much more than a witch or demigod was beyond me—especially with the golden crown of the Greek Week champion on his head.

The same could be said of Vera, who was wearing a short, white cocktail dress that flared out at the bottom, with a neckline that dipped low between her breasts. Instead of a descendent of Aphrodite, she looked like she could be the goddess of love herself.

She and Zane looked upon us as if they were our rulers, and we were their subjects. Which was, of course, exactly what they believed was true.

Everyone stood and clapped at their entrance. Even Kate, Blake, and Nicole looked mesmerized by their presence.

Zane glanced at me with empty eyes, then quickly looked away. He appeared as ambivalent about me as he was about everyone else in the room. If I didn't know any better, I would have believed it was true.

Kate lifted her champagne and surveyed the crowd. "Now, for the toast," she said, and I swallowed down the anxiety in my throat, bracing myself for the madness that was about to begin.

CHAPTER TWENTY-ONE

Everyone else reached for their glasses and held them up.

My hand moved automatically to do the same. As my fingers wrapped around it, I felt like I was watching my movements from somewhere else—not doing them myself.

I should say something. Stop everyone from drinking the poisoned champagne before it was too late.

But then I pictured everyone in the room turning on Zane and Vera, attacking them until their blood stained the ground and their eyes stared emptily up at the ceiling.

Horror pulled at my throat at the image, blocking any words from escaping.

The mead won't hurt them, I reminded myself. *It'll just make it feel like they drank way more than one glass of champagne.*

The most pain they'd experience would be a nasty hangover tomorrow morning.

Everything was going to be okay.

Unfortunately, thinking it wasn't making me believe it.

I glanced at Zane, sucking in a sharp breath of surprise at the sight of his eyes boring into mine. He was totally still, and even though he was across the room, I could practically feel the mental support he was trying to send my way.

I could have sworn I felt Mason studying me as well, but I refused to look over at him. I didn't want to give him the slightest bit of attention that might be misconstrued as interest.

At some point, Kate had started speaking. Stuff about how it had been a difficult time recently, but that the focus we'd put into training this past week was proof that we could take on whatever was thrown at us.

"Aièn aristeúein," she finished in Greek. "Ever to excel."

She raised her glass to her lips.

I froze, half-expecting her to smell the champagne, scrunch her face in confusion, say there was something wrong with it, and warn everyone not to drink it.

But she took a sip, clueless that anything was wrong.

Everyone else in the room followed. Some students took small sips, while others managed to finish the entire glass in one go. But, just as Zane and Vera had promised, everyone had at least a bit of it.

Not wanting to stand out in the crowd, I pretended to take a sip. But I was careful to not let the champagne touch my lips. Afterward, I put the glass back down on the table and yanked my hand away from it like I was avoiding a poisonous snake.

The DJ started the music again, and people hurried to the dance floor, surrounding Zane and Vera with their excitement and congratulations. Now that Zane was "king," everyone wanted to be his new best friend.

"Not a fan of champagne?" Mason asked.

Crap.

Did he realize I hadn't drank any?

"I'm not a big drinker," I said quickly. "One sip is enough for me."

He studied me and took another sip from his glass, savoring it in a way that made the simple act of drinking champagne look sexual.

I wasn't sure if he was aware of it, or if it just came naturally to him.

"Then that means more for the rest of us." He grinned and looked out to the already packed dance floor. "I take it you don't want to dance?"

"I most definitely don't." It wasn't even because I didn't want to dance with him. I just didn't like dancing.

"I'm more of a 'sit at the side of the room and chat with a friend' type of person."

"Your loss." He placed his now-empty glass on the table and swaggered to the dance floor, students parting around him to let him past.

The music got louder, and the smell of sweet champagne lingered in the air, a reminder of the poison I'd watched everyone consume without lifting a finger to warn them.

More people made their way to the dance floor, giggling and unsteady on their feet. Nicole and Blake danced with barely any space between them, their eyes locked, looking at each other like they wanted to rip each other's clothes off in front of everyone. Another couple started making out, his hand on her thigh, inching up and disappearing up her dress. Even Kate was getting into it, singing into her now-empty champagne glass like it was a microphone.

Wow. That mead worked *quickly*.

"Summer!" Jamie slurred, grabbing my hand. "Come dance with us!"

Topher slung his arm around her shoulders, looking more relaxed than I'd ever seen him.

"I'm gonna get more food," I lied. "I'll see you out there in a bit."

"Sounds good!" She released my hand and stumbled with Topher onto the dance floor.

"Are you drinking that?" Penny asked from across the table, pointing to my champagne.

"I'm done," I moved away from it further.

"Can I have it?"

I wanted to tell her no. But that would look sketchy, since I'd just said I was done with it.

"Are you sure?" I asked instead. "It tasted kind of strong."

"Yes!" She took the champagne and drank it like it was the nectar of the gods, smiling in ultimate pleasure. "I think you should talk to Zane tonight," she said after a few sips. "I think he likes you."

No kidding.

"I think he does, too." I blew out a long breath and watched Zane slither off the dance floor, heading toward the back doors where he'd entered.

Vera was only a bit behind him.

Everyone was so drunk off the mead that they didn't seem to notice. Even the guy behind the DJ booth was standing with his hands in the air, amping up the crowd as if he was the star performer at the hottest club in Miami.

"I'm *starving*," Penny said suddenly, and she spun around and hurried to the buffet, where a bunch of other students were filling up their plates as high as possible.

My watched buzzed with a text, and I raised it to see what it said.

It was from Vera.

You coming?

An excellent question.

Was I truly going to go through with helping them with this? It had all happened so quickly that I didn't feel like I'd had enough time to fully think it through.

But it was now or never.

So I did another survey of the sloppy, wasted crowd, took a deep breath, and made my decision.

CHAPTER TWENTY-TWO

I crept toward the back exit of the gym, looking over my shoulder every few seconds.

No one noticed me leaving. They were too caught up in whatever vice they were indulging in—dancing, food, each other—to have any interest in me.

It was just like Vera had promised.

I reached the exit, did one last glance over my shoulder, then headed out the door.

I gasped, immediately assaulted by the freezing cold air.

"Jacket?" someone said from next to me.

Zane. He was standing outside the door, offering me his blazer.

"No." My teeth chattered, my breath fogging in front of my face. "I'm fine."

He tilted his head, amused. "Are you sure about that?"

A breeze blew past us, making it feel at least ten degrees colder than before.

"No," I gave in, and he handed over the blazer, his fingers brushing mine in the process.

Despite his lower-than-normal body temperature, my skin heated at his touch.

I slipped on the blazer, not looking at him as I did so. It was lined with something warm and fuzzy—something that made my arms feel surprisingly warm.

"I had it lined with merino wool," he said simply. "I knew you'd be cold tonight, and that you'd need it. Wool is one of the best materials to regulate body temperate."

"Oh," I said. "That was... thoughtful."

"I try." He smiled, his teeth sharp and deadly. "You'll also need this." He removed a dagger from his belt and offered it to me.

"Thanks." I took it and held onto it, since I didn't have anywhere on my dress to stow it.

It warmed as it responded to me, like the metal weapons I'd held so far.

Vera cleared her throat—I'd been so wrapped up in Zane that I hadn't even realized she was standing there. "We have to go," she declared, and she spun around, leading us away from the gym.

The music got quieter, and soon, we were all the way across campus, approaching the forest.

Everything bad seemed to happen near the forest.

"Where are we going?" I asked.

She huffed, and even though her back was toward me, I imagined she was rolling her eyes. "We're going to kill Fulla."

"I know that," I snapped. "I didn't ask what we were doing. I asked where we were going."

"They're keeping her in a storm shelter at the edge of the woods, just beyond where it meets the lake," Zane said before Vera could answer.

"Near where we had the memorial ceremony?" I asked.

"Yep."

I shuddered at the realization that we'd been so close to Fulla while we'd been saying goodbye to our fallen classmates.

Eventually, I felt a sudden awareness of metal. Vera stopped next to the place where the metal felt the strongest, kneeled, and brushed dead leaves off a storm shelter buried in the ground. It was the kind with metal doors facing the sky that I'd seen in various tornado movies, a thick chain with a large padlock binding the handles together.

"Let me guess," I said. "You want me to open the lock."

"It's been strengthened with magic." Vera stepped back and motioned to the padlock. "Do your best."

I placed my freezing cold hand over it—the one that

wasn't gripping the dagger. The metal was so cold that it should have frozen my skin, but instead, my hand warmed it as the magic flowed through me.

On instinct, I reached into the lock with my magic and felt the grooves where the key would go. It only took a simple pressing of them with my mind to click the lock open.

"Brilliant." Vera pushed me out of the way, removed the lock from the doors, and tossed it to the ground. Then she opened the doors, her hungry eyes gazing down the steps that led beneath the ground. "Let's go."

I glanced at Zane.

"Go ahead." He stood back so I could go down after Vera.

I peered down the stairs and had a sudden flashback of walking down to the speakeasy with Alyssa. Except unlike the speakeasy, these stairs were old and lit by dim bulbs hanging from the ceiling.

I tightened my grip on the dagger and hesitantly started down. It smelled like mildew, and the air warmed now that there was no wind.

Zane followed behind me, pulling the doors closed after he was fully in the stairwell.

The air inside was now totally still. Trapping me. Like it was a black hole trying to eat me alive.

My breathing echoed through the stairwell, and my chest tightened with nerves.

"Summer?" Zane said my name cautiously. "Are you okay?"

My gaze locked with his, the sight of his caring eyes grounding me. I stilled, locked in place, and heated desire for him consumed me.

From the intense way he was looking at me, I knew he felt the same.

"She's fine," Vera snipped from the bottom of the stairs. "Are you guys coming?"

"Yeah." I forced my gaze away from Zane's and hurried down the rest of the stairs.

We joined Vera at the bottom—a small room with what looked like a bank vault door on the opposite wall. As I glanced around, my eyes stopped at the cameras attached to the top corners of the ceiling.

"Don't worry about those," Vera said. "I've already taken care of them."

Of course she had.

The same way she'd taken care of the buildings my watch allowed me to access.

"Here's your second challenge." She motioned to the vault, which was huge and imposing—and made of pure metal.

"How'd you know this would be here if you couldn't get through the first doors?" I asked.

"Technology." She motioned to the cameras overhead. "I told you I'm good with it."

"You tapped into the system."

"I did."

I studied the vault, thinking. "How many doors are there beyond this one?" I asked.

"This is the last of them," she said. "There's a prison behind it with a few cells. Fulla's in one of them."

"Who's in the others?"

"They're empty."

"Which is a good thing," Zane added. "Because we won't have any witnesses."

From his tone, I had a feeling that if there had been witnesses, they might have been on the immortals' hitlist as well.

"Let me guess," I said. "You need me to open Fulla's cell, too?"

"Your magic is quite useful," Vera said simply.

"Glad to be of service." I gave her a fake smile to accentuate the sarcasm dripping from my tone, then walked over to the vaulted door. It had a big wheel-thing in the center with spokes coming out of it to grab, and a gigantic combination lock below it.

"Well?" Vera crossed her arms impatiently. "Are you going to open it?"

"Give me a second." I held the center knob of the lock, closed my eyes, and reached out to the mechanism inside it with my magic. I searched for something to press—like I had with the padlock—but nothing happened.

"Turn it," Zane suggested. "Try to feel where it clicks into place."

"Okay." It was worth a shot. So, I closed my eyes and turned the dial right.

Just like Zane predicted, I felt the place where it clicked into place. Well, more like the spot where the notch on the first wheel lined up with the pin at the top.

Focusing harder, I sensed that there were four wheels inside the combination lock, and I spun the dial back and forth until each one lined up with the pin. The mechanism was pretty simple. I didn't even know which numbers I was landing on—I had my eyes closed the entire time and could simply *feel* where to stop.

Now that they were all lined up, I opened my eyes and reached for one of the spokes on the wheel. Taking a deep breath, I rotated it and opened the door, revealing a bare room with a few jail cells in it.

A woman in sweatpants and a t-shirt sat on the bed in the center cell. But despite her simple clothes, she had an ethereal glow to her, with dewy skin and long blonde hair that shined like it had been freshly blown dry.

"Fulla," Vera said, prowling forward like a cat to stand in front of the cell.

Hope crossed the goddess's features, and she smiled. "I was wondering when someone was going to come to break me out of here," she said.

Of course—she had no way of knowing that Zane and Vera had turned on her.

"You're definitely not going to be in here much longer." Vera glanced over her shoulder and looked at Zane. "You should do the honors. You are, after all, the reason we ended up in this position."

"Very well." He approached Fulla's cell, his back now toward me. If he had any doubts about what he was about to do, his body language didn't show it. "This should only take a second."

In a flash, he removed the dagger from his belt and launched it in a straight shot toward Fulla.

It struck her perfectly in the heart.

But I didn't have time to see her turn to ash.

Because Vera spun around and ran toward me, a sharp icicle raised in her hand, and her pale blue eyes blazing with murder.

CHAPTER TWENTY-THREE

I somehow gathered enough common sense to *move*.
But Vera slammed into me, threw me to the ground, and aimed the icicle at my heart.

I squirmed out of the way, but the place between my collarbone and shoulder numbed with cold, ice rushing through my veins.

I sucked in a sharp, painful breath, realizing she must have stabbed my shoulder with the icicle. It was smart. Metal couldn't hurt me, but ice could.

But despite the cold, one place in my body was still warm.

My hand.

Because my fingers were still wrapped tightly around the dagger Zane had given me earlier.

So, I summoned all the strength I had—gathering a huge amount of it from the dagger—and stabbed the blade through Vera's heart before she could come back down on me.

Zane had flashed over at some point, wrapping his hands so tightly around Vera's neck that she couldn't release a sound. He let out a low, agonized scream, squeezing her neck tighter and tighter until her dead eyes started popping out of their sockets.

I would have gagged at the sight, but I was too light-headed to do much of anything except release my hold on my dagger, my arm flopping to the floor.

Zane threw Vera's body down next to me, then collapsed to his knees, pressing his hands over the wound to put pressure on it and slow the bleeding.

I couldn't see my shoulder, but I'd felt Vera's icicle penetrate it.

My brain felt hazy, my body so cold that I could barely feel anything at all.

I was going to die.

Despite having already faced the fury, the troll, the handmaiden in the woods, and even Lincoln, it hadn't set in yet that in all those situations, I could have died. Well, a part of my mind had known, but it hadn't felt *real*, since I'd always escaped the danger.

"It's bad, isn't it?" I somehow managed to ask.

"It is," he said, as confident and determined as ever. "But you're going to be okay."

Empty promises.

My head spun, dizzy. I was so cold now that my teeth had stopped chattering.

"I guess I'll finally get to meet my father," I said, the words barely able to escape my frozen lips.

Suddenly, Zane held the edge of his dagger to his wrist and sliced it open, drawing blood. He thrust his wrist up against my lips, his expression hard, and said, "Drink."

His blood dripped into my mouth, and I had no option but to do as he commanded. It tasted salty and metallic, and even though his body temperature ran cold, his blood was warm. It coated my throat and traveled down to my stomach, and I wasn't as cold anymore, and my head stopped feeling so woozy and light.

I wanted to drink forever. But eventually, he pulled his wrist away, and his skin repaired itself until the cut disappeared.

I propped myself up and inspected the place where the icicle had speared my shoulder.

There was no wound. But blood had pooled on my skin, and it had puddled around me on the floor.

I reached for the place where the wound should have been, sure it must be some sort of hallucination, but it the skin was smooth and unbroken.

As I tried to process what had just happened, I surveyed everything around me.

Fulla had been reduced to a pile of ashes in the locked jail cell.

Vera was rolled over, staring blankly at the ceiling with dead, bulging eyes, my dagger protruding out of her chest. Bright red blood stained her white dress around it.

Zane reached for the dagger, pulled it out of her chest, and handed it to me. "Here," he said flatly. "This is yours."

"You loaned it to me," I replied, unable to look away from Vera's mangled corpse. "It's yours."

"You killed with it. It belongs to you now."

Knowing that what he was saying was true, I reached forward and accepted the dagger. The metal hummed in my hand, like it was agreeing that it was mine.

Of course it was. *All* metal was mine.

I kept my eyes locked on Zane's as the power rushed through me. "You healed me with your blood," I said, surprised at how steady I sounded through my shock. "Like some sort of... vampire."

"I'm not a vampire." He chuckled, his serious demeanor from a few seconds ago gone.

"Then how did you do that?"

He pressed his lips together, and I sat completely still, silent as I waited for him to answer my question.

But before he could, the vault door swung open wider, and Mason stepped through.

I froze, expecting him to be shocked, or angry, or both.

Instead, he stood there quietly, observing the scene in front of him.

My hand tightened around the dagger, ready to use it if necessary. I didn't want to, but what if Mason attacked, like Vera had?

And if he didn't, how were we supposed to explain all of this?

Before I could even start to think of an answer, Zane jumped to his feet, looking ready to do whatever it took to defend himself.

To defend *us*.

On instinct, I reached for the vault door with my mind and used my magic to push it closed. It was heavy, but after whatever Zane had just done to me, I felt stronger than ever.

The lock clicked back into place.

We were locked in here.

Specifically: *Mason* was locked in here.

Because I could use my magic to get us out whenever I pleased. And I most certainly didn't want Mason leaving and telling the others what he'd walked in on.

Zane nodded at me in approval, somehow managing to keep watch on Mason at the same time, ready to pounce whenever necessary.

Mason, however, didn't move to attack.

"Well." Mason broke the silence, smirking as he glanced at Fulla's ashes. "I don't know what I was expecting, but I have to give you credit, because it certainly wasn't *this* impressive turn of events."

CHAPTER TWENTY-FOUR

"Impressive?" I repeated, completely and utterly caught off-guard by his reaction.

"That creature that was in there was the enemy." He motioned to the pile of ashes that used to be Fulla. "Which means the three of you evaluated an opportunity—the ball where everyone else was inebriated—then somehow sneaked in here and killed her. Well, the two of you managed to do this. I see things didn't work out well for Vera." He glanced at her body, thoroughly undisturbed by the fact that one of the students at the academy was laying on the floor *dead*.

"She attacked me," I said. "She tried to kill me. I defended myself."

"I see." Mason tilted his head thoughtfully. "She always *was* jealous of your relationship with Zane."

"We're not in a relationship," I said quickly. "But yes—she was jealous."

Maybe not romantically, but she didn't like that I'd taken Zane's attention away from her. And as twisted as it was, I *did* think it was one of the reasons she'd attacked me.

That, along with the fact that she didn't trust me with her and Zane's secret.

"The solution to this problem is simple," Mason continued, still disturbingly blasé. "We have to hide the body."

"Wait." I couldn't believe what I'd just heard. *"What?"*

"You can't expect us to actually believe you want to help us," Zane said coolly, holding his dagger at the ready.

Ready to kill Mason.

"Since we find ourselves in such an interesting situation, I think it's best to get this over with." Mason zeroed in on Zane. "You and Vera aren't the only immortals at this school."

Zane's body tensed. "You're one of us."

"I am." He turned his palm to the ceiling and created an ice crystal that floated a few inches above his hand.

My mouth nearly dropped open in shock.

"You should have told us," Zane said.

"I wasn't sent here to work with you," he said simply. "I'm here to watch out for you."

Zane's expression darkened. "You're spying on us."

"Correct." Mason smirked. "After I realized you'd spiked the mead, I figured you were up to something. So, I followed you here, and the rest is history."

"How much did you hear?" Zane asked.

"All of it. And I must say, it was about time you took care of Fulla. I was starting to wonder if you were up to the task. Although this does lead to an interesting question," he said, focusing on me. "How, exactly, do you fit in to all of this?"

"She's my soulmate." Zane stepped in front of me, as if to protect me. "Which means she's under our protection."

"She's Greek." Mason sneered, as if it made me vermin. "That's impossible."

"I didn't say I could explain why it happened," Zane said. "But apparently, it's possible. We wouldn't be here otherwise."

"It's true," I spoke in Zane's defense.

Mason sized me up. "Interesting," he finally said. "Are you sure you're not Norse?"

"I'm sure," I said, since my mom had confirmed it in the cottage. "But there's something big here that doesn't add up."

"Which is…" Mason trailed, as if he already knew what I was thinking.

"I've seen you use air magic," I said. "But as far as I'm aware, immortals don't *have* air magic."

"We don't," Zane confirmed, his eyes not leaving Mason.

"Let's just say it has something to do with my gift, and leave it at that," he said. "But we don't have time for this right now. We need to get rid of Vera's body and Fulla's ashes. With both gone, it'll look like Vera snuck in here during the ball and freed Fulla. No one will look for them on campus if they think they left."

"That was some pretty fast thinking," Zane said.

"What can I say?" Mason gave Zane his signature smirk. "I'm quick on my feet. But—before we get started—there's one more thing I need from you. From *both* of you."

"What's that?" I stilled, bracing myself for anything. Because while Mason might be on Zane's side, he wasn't on mine.

Soulmate bond with Zane or not, as far as Mason was concerned, I was the enemy.

"I'll help you clean up this mess and cover it up—which is the only way you'll be able to possibly get out of it. But in return, you're going to owe me a favor."

"What sort of favor?" Zane asked, immediately on guard.

"To be determined." He grinned, confident we wouldn't say no.

"Are you sure you're an immortal and not a fae?" I asked.

"What?" Mason's brow creased in confusion. So did Zane's.

"Nothing," I brushed it off, since from what I'd learned at the academy so far, fae were only a thing of fiction. Then I turned to Zane, since he was one of the masterminds of this botched plan. "What do you think?"

"I highly recommend taking me up on this," Mason said to Zane—as if I wasn't in the room with them. "We wouldn't want word to get out to our people that you stood by while a Greek killed one of our own, would you?"

Zane didn't even flinch. "We most certainly wouldn't." He held Mason's predatory gaze with his own. "I'll accept your offer."

"The right decision." Mason walked to a small door on the side of the room and opened it, revealing what looked to be a janitor's closet. "Gotta keep cleaning supplies around in an underground holding and torture facility," he said. "Who wants to sweep, and who wants to take care of the blood?"

"I'll sweep," I volunteered, since the thought of cleaning up Vera's blood made me gag.

Plus, as I'd just learned, Zane was the expert with blood around here.

There was *so much* I needed to talk with him about.

Later. I'd get to it later. Right now, we had more

important things to focus on—such as cleaning up the scene of a double murder.

There were enough supplies in the closet that once we were done, there were no signs that anything had taken place here. There were no signs that anyone had even *been* here.

"I'll take care of restocking later," Mason said, closing the door. "Now, we have to get the ashes and body out of here."

The way he referred to Vera chilled me. Not as a person who'd just died. Just as *a body.*

Zane was completely robotic as he picked up Vera's limp, bloodied corpse and maneuvered her around his shoulders so he could carry her on his back.

Mason walked over to get the bucket of Fulla's ashes, but I picked it up first. "It's fine," I said. "I've got it."

He nodded in approval.

Zane led the way out of the underground shelter, and I followed with the bucket, trying my hardest not to look at Vera's body flopped over Zane's shoulders. Mason went last, locking the vault and entry doors behind us. He ensured the padlock was secure, and then we walked silently to the frozen lake.

I shivered, unable to wrap my arms around myself to keep warm, since I was holding the bucket of ashes.

Finally, we reached the edge of the lake, and Mason

motioned to the ice. "Should you do the honors, or should I?" he asked Zane.

Confusion passed through me. Because how could Mason do anything to the ice?

Then I remembered—he was an immortal. Which meant he had ice magic.

It was going to take a bit to get used to that.

"I've got it." Zane placed Vera's body on the ground, not looking at it, and kneeled to lean over the ice. Just like the water elemental had done during the funeral ceremony, he melted a circle of it beneath his hand.

A circle wide enough to dump in a body feet-first.

His eyes were hollow and dead as he looked down at it.

Mason was already at work removing Vera's dress from her body and ripping it into pieces to use to tie sacks of rocks around her ankles.

I turned my head. Because even though Vera had tried to kill me, it felt too disrespectful to watch this being done to her. Instead, I picked up some rocks and dumped them into the bucket of Fulla's ashes to make sure it would fully sink.

Zane picked Vera's body up again, and I dropped the bucket with Fulla's ashes into the dark depths of the lake. It didn't take long before it was gone from sight.

I was gazing down into the watery abyss when someone said my name.

Zane.

"I need to finish this," he continued.

"Right." I swallowed, took a deep breath of the icy air, and stepped to the side.

The air stung my lungs, and I realized I'd been in so much shock that I'd barely registered how cold it was.

As I watched Zane lower Vera's body into the lake, I couldn't believe this was happening.

We were covering up a murder.

A murder that *I'd* committed.

I felt like I'd crossed over to the dark side, and there was no going back.

After a few seconds, Zane kneeled back down and used his magic to seal the lake. The ice he'd created blended in with that around it—there was nothing to show that it had been disturbed.

"There." Zane stared at the ice, not speaking to either of us in particular. "It's done."

"Not quite yet," Mason said, his tone surprisingly chipper given what we'd been up to. "We still have to make sure we're not placed at the scene of the crime."

"Isn't that why we gave them the mead?" I asked.

"The mead will make their memories and sense of time foggy," he said. "But it'll be best to make our alibis as airtight as we can. Which means we should go back to the ball. The two of you can come out of the back together, holding hands and looking cozy. Make a big show of leaving out the main doors together. And then you need to be seen leaving Zane's room tomorrow morning." He zeroed in on me at that last part. "Nothing you haven't done before."

I narrowed my eyes at him, refusing to look at Zane. "Is there another option?" I asked.

"Can you think of anything better?"

I tried to wrack my mind for something, but came up with nothing.

From the steely look in Zane's eyes, he agreed with Mason that this was our best move.

"You can have the bed." There was sadness in Zane's tone, so deep that it nearly broke my heart. "I don't mind."

"Thank you," I said, and I straightened, trying to prepare myself for the crazy show we were about to put on. "Now, I guess we should do this and get it over with."

CHAPTER TWENTY-FIVE

Somehow, I blocked out all emotion as Zane and I emerged from the back of the gym like a couple that had taken some space to make out and was now overcome with desire to leave the party together.

It wasn't real. I was just playing a role.

As long as I told myself that, it felt like I was living someone else's life and not my own.

People watched us leave together, some of them cheering and congratulating Zane for having the true win of the evening.

I was too detached from the situation to tell them to mind their own business. Plus, the more people who noticed us, the stronger our alibi. It was the entire point of us doing this.

There were a few other students walking back along the main paths, so Zane kept his arm around me to maintain the charade. Despite everything, I leaned into him, grateful for any feeling of comfort that I could get after everything that had just happened.

It didn't take long until we were back at the water dorm.

The last time I'd been here, it had been to visit Vera.

Little did anyone else know, she was never going to return to her room again.

Neither of us said a word as we walked down the hall and into his room. It looked just as I remembered, as pristine and neat as always.

He shut the door behind me, and I spun around to face him, furious as all the emotions I'd felt all evening flooded to the surface. "Your blood can heal," I started, still unable to believe it, even though I'd seen it happen. "All of those students who were injured by the handmaidens... Alyssa... the two of you could have healed them. The three of you," I added, remembering that Mason was immortal, too.

"Vera and Mason couldn't have done anything," he said. "I'm the only one of us who can heal."

"Your gift," I realized.

"Yes. My gift." He held his gaze with mine, ready for the onslaught.

"It doesn't matter. Because *you* could have healed them," I repeated, since that was the important part. "But you did absolutely nothing." Hatred leaked from my tone.

Because that was what I was feeling—total and absolute hatred.

How could this *monster* be my soulmate?

And how was I not going to Kate and telling her everything right now?

The unfortunate answer was that even though it was crazy, I still couldn't bring myself to hurt him. And after helping them kill Fulla, I was too deeply involved to turn back.

"If I healed them, I'd expose myself," he said calmly. "We both know I can't do that."

I pressed my lips together, since it was true. And Zane wasn't the type of hero who would put his people at risk to help the students here.

Zane wasn't a hero at all.

"Give me some of your blood," I said, feeling like my mind was moving at a million miles per second. "Put it in a container or something. I'll bring it to the infirmary and give it to Alyssa. No one will know it had anything to do with you."

"We can't leave right now," he said, as detached from the conversation as he'd been since I'd killed Vera. "If anyone sees us leaving the dorm, it will ruin our alibi. Besides, my gift doesn't work that way. To heal someone, my blood has to be drank straight from the source."

The source.

As in, it had to be drank directly from him.

"That's why Nicole was able to heal Drake and Topher after you injured them in the competitions," I realized. "The blood on their lips. That was yours."

"Yes." He nodded. "I cut myself and put my blood on their lips, moving quickly enough that no one would notice, including them. I was the one who healed them—not Nicole."

"And you're going to heal Alyssa. We'll go to the infirmary tomorrow morning," I said. "I've visited her enough that it won't look suspicious. You'll heal her, and she'll wake up."

"Deal," he said.

I paused, waiting for him to add a condition to it. But all he did was wait for my reply.

"Really?" I asked, surprised he'd agreed so easily.

"You've done so much for me," he said. "Healing Alyssa is the least I can do to thank you."

"I'm not keeping your secret to help *you*," I said without thinking.

"Then who are you doing it for?"

I stared at him, and it was so silent in the room that I could almost hear my heart pounding. "I'm doing it for me," I said, softly and slowly. "Because I can't handle the pain of thinking about hurting you."

When I said it that way, I sounded so weak.

I hated myself for it.

I hated myself for a lot of things nowadays.

"It's because of the soulmate bond," he said simply. "We're wired to help our soulmates, no matter what."

"Even if it means helping them cover up a murder."

"Yes." His eyes darkened. "Even if it means covering up a murder." He broke his gaze with mine and walked to his drawers, pulling out a large t-shirt and flannel pants that looked like the ones my mom and I wore on Christmas. "Here." He held it out to me. "For you to sleep in."

I wanted to say no—that I could sleep in my own clothes. But this dress was far from the most comfortable thing in the world. And my only other option was to sleep in my bra and underwear.

So, Zane's t-shirt and flannel pants it was. At least the pants had a drawstring, so I'd kind of be able to get them to fit.

"Thanks." I took them from him and went into his bathroom to change and freshen up.

When I met my gaze in the mirror, I was startled by how hollow my eyes looked.

They were the eyes of someone who'd just killed.

The prickling sensation of being watched started, and I hurried back to Zane's room. Because even though I didn't know who was watching me, I didn't want them to see me like this.

When I walked in, Zane was mid-way through changing, wearing only his boxers.

I sucked in a sharp breath, unable to move my eyes

away from his perfectly chiseled abs. He was all long lines and lean muscle, every crevice on his body carved to perfection. My stomach warmed, my cheeks were on fire, and I found myself unable to form words.

The corner of his lips lifted into a small smile. "Like what you see?" he asked.

"Yes," I said, and then I quickly corrected myself. "No. Can you put a shirt on?"

My body was reacting so insanely crazy to him that I worried if he didn't put a shirt on, this would turn into what everyone at the academy assumed was happening in here right now.

This was ridiculous. I seriously needed to get ahold of myself.

So I faced the corner of the room, aware of Zane's every movement as he pulled his shirt over his head.

"There," he said once he was done. "Better?"

I turned back around.

No, my thoughts betrayed me.

"Yes," I said instead, although from the twinkle in his eyes, I could tell he didn't believe me.

But he stepped closer to me, seriousness replacing the slight bit of happiness.

"When you thought you were dying, you said you were going to be with your father now," he said. "What did you mean by that?"

Right—Zane still didn't know I was the daughter of Hades. He wasn't supposed to know.

But we already shared so many secrets. And keeping secrets was exhausting me.

I might as well tell him the truth.

So, feeling awkward standing in the middle of his room, I walked over to his bed and sat down.

He—thankfully—remained standing.

"Hades is my father." I figured I might as well get to the point. "He's the god of metal and gems. It's why I can control them."

"I suspected as much," Zane said, and he sat on the couch—not the bed.

An intentional choice.

One to make sure I felt comfortable.

Why did he have to be so considerate? Resisting him would be a lot easier if he could just act like the jerk he'd claimed to be outside the cafeteria that day when he'd lied and told me he'd been drunk the first night we'd spent together.

"So why didn't you say anything?" I asked.

"Because it's your secret, for you to tell me when—or if—you're ready," he said. "Besides, I don't care who your father is. I only care about *you*."

The way he emphasized that final word took my breath away. Because it was like he was speaking from his soul, promising he'd always protect me, no matter what.

And as much as I hated to admit it, I knew deep inside myself that he truly would.

"Thanks," I said, hoping to diffuse the tension. "Keeping all these secrets is exhausting."

"Tell me about it." He blew out a slow breath and stared at the wall, looking deep in thought.

In that moment, he looked so incredibly human. It was hard to believe he was the same sharp-eyed immortal I'd talked to in the boat, when he'd told me his plans about why he was infiltrating the school.

"Are you doing okay?" I asked cautiously. "You've known Vera for a long time…"

And I killed her.

The words were on the tip of my tongue, but I couldn't say them.

Because I'd *killed* someone. It wasn't like when I'd killed the troll. Vera was a person. She and Zane had been life-long friends. And now, she was gone.

"Hey." Zane stood up, walked over, and sat down on the bed next to me. "It's not your fault."

"Except it *is* my fault," I said. "I could have stabbed her somewhere else. I didn't have to go for the heart."

"She was about to kill you," he said. "Even if she hadn't gotten that final shot through the heart, the first injury she gave you *would* have killed you if I hadn't been there to save you. You did what you had to in order to survive. Anyone would have done the same."

I flashed back to the murderous look in Vera's eyes when she'd hovered over me, about to take that final strike. Did I really have to kill her? If I'd stabbed her somewhere non-fatal, would it have given Zane enough time to stop her from killing me, and to heal me?

Maybe. I'd never know.

But even if Zane had stopped her and saved me, it wouldn't change the fact that Vera had tried to kill me. If she were alive, I'd never be safe on campus.

"Maybe." I shrugged, knowing he was right. "But still—she was your friend. I'm sorry."

No words felt like they could be enough for what I was apologizing for. I'd never be able to forgive *myself* for it.

I supposed all that was possible would be acceptance. And I imagined it would take a while to get there.

"Thanks." His eyes hardened, and I could tell he was hurting. It was the same way he'd looked when he'd lowered Vera into the lake. He was in pain. A *lot* of it. And, for the first time, he looked like he felt lost and alone.

Again, I was struck by how human his emotions were.

Maybe he wasn't the monster I thought he was.

"You don't have to sleep on the couch tonight," I said, overtaken by a wave of sympathy—and boldness—that took me by surprise.

"You're my guest," he said. "You're sleeping on the bed."

"I never said I wouldn't."

My breaths shallowed, and he watched me cautiously, like he was afraid I was going to take the offer back.

"Are you sure?" His eyes traveled up and down my body—not like he could see much in the oversized t-shirt I was wearing.

This could be a really bad idea, I thought.

But despite knowing that, I hated the thought of him trying to sleep all squished in that small couch after what he'd been through tonight.

After what we'd *both* been through tonight.

There was also no denying that I'd get something out of this, too. Because even right now, sitting next to him, I felt a sense of safety and comfort that I hadn't had since being back home with my mom.

And, above all of that, he'd saved my life tonight. He was trusting me with secrets that could spell out his death if anyone found them out. I felt so alarmingly close to him, despite having a million reasons why I shouldn't.

"We'll just sleep," I said. "Nothing else."

"Sure," he said. "Sounds good."

From the hypnotizing way he was looking at me, I knew that if I made any moves to do something *other* than sleeping, he wouldn't say no.

But he was also respectful. I trusted him.

"Cool." I swallowed, wanting to be as relaxed as possible, even though I felt anything but relaxed. But I *was* tired, and I yawned at the realization of the exhaustion that had crept up on me.

Zane leaned back, and I noticed how close we'd been sitting before. "You lost a lot a blood earlier," he said. "You should get some sleep."

"Yeah. I should," I said, although I made no move to do so. "And Zane?"

"Yeah?" He stilled, waiting for whatever I had to say.

"Thank you."

"For what?"

"For saving my life."

With that, I crawled under the covers, curled away from him to face the wall, and closed my eyes to go to sleep.

CHAPTER TWENTY-SIX

I was aware of Zane's every move as he got ready for bed and crawled under the covers next to me. But I pretended I was already asleep, because after everything we'd been through tonight, we both needed time to process what had happened.

As I lay there, I couldn't help but count every one of his breaths. Was he asleep, or was he lying there thinking, like I was?

Eventually I drifted off, then woke the next morning to the soft light of dawn peeking through the window.

Zane wasn't in the bed, but the shower was running in his bathroom.

I took the liberty of helping myself to a can of Coke in his mini-fridge and contemplated whether I should change back into my dress or keep his t-shirt and pants on. Either would be equally damning to walk back in. But his t-shirt would make it even more obvious that I was with him last night, and since our alibi was that we'd been hooking up in his room, t-shirt it was.

The shower stopped, and after a few minutes, Zane came out of the bathroom—fully dressed. He must have brought his clothes in there to change into, so he wouldn't make things awkward for me in here.

The image of walking in on him half-naked last night flashed through my mind. My cheeks heated at the memory, and I pulled my gaze away from him, not wanting to stare.

"Everyone on campus will still be sleeping right now," he said. "We'll go to the infirmary, heal Alyssa, then come back here." He opened one of his drawers and pulled out a black sweatshirt. "Put this on so you don't freeze."

I did as instructed, then put my boots from last night back on, dressing in silence.

Sleeping in the bed with him had felt more intimate than I'd expected. I wasn't sure, but I could have sworn he'd wrapped his arms around me at some point. Or maybe I'd just been dreaming.

As my thoughts drifted, my gaze went to my dagger sitting on top of his nightstand. On a whim, I took it and tucked it into the inside of my right boot. It was a bit loose in there, but the sharp edges wouldn't be able to cut through my skin, and I'd have relatively easy access if I needed it.

"Thanks again for doing this," I told Zane once I was ready.

"Anytime," he said, and then he opened his door, and we left his room.

Just as Zane had said, no one was awake. It was like a sleeping spell had been cast over the campus.

The infirmary was quiet as well. There was supposed to be a nurse at the front desk at all times, but it was empty.

Trying to be as quiet as possible, I opened the door to Alyssa's room. She was lying in bed, eyes closed, hooked up to the machines that were keeping her alive. The swelling in her face was going down, but she was as still as ever.

"Your dagger." Zane held out his hand, although he was looking at Alyssa and not at me.

I pulled the dagger out of my boot, handed it to him, and he moved to stand by Alyssa's side.

I followed him, standing so close that my arm brushed his.

Electricity buzzed through me.

From the way his breath hitched, he felt the same thing. But he remained focused on Alyssa, not so much as glancing at me.

He brought the dagger to his palm and sliced diagonally, leaving a trail of blood in the blade's path. He didn't even wince. Then he held his hand over Alyssa's lips, made a fist, and squeezed so the blood dripped down into her mouth.

She remained still.

Could the blood heal her if she wasn't able to swallow it?

Zane squeezed his hand tighter, and I held my breath, waiting for something to happen.

After a few seconds, she swallowed.

I leaned forward on the bed, my heart feeling like it was going to burst with anticipation. "It's working," I said softly, watching as color crept onto her pale face. The bruises that had been there faded and disappeared.

She reached for Zane's hand and pulled it closer to her mouth, sucking his blood as if it were more delicious than the rarest wine on the planet. Her eyes remained tightly closed the entire time.

If it hurt Zane at all, he didn't let it show.

Eventually, he drew his hand out of her grasp, and he handed the dagger back to me.

I slipped it back inside my boot, which I felt was quickly becoming its new home.

Before I could right myself, he grabbed my hand and pulled me out of the room.

I glanced over my shoulder and saw Alyssa stirring, but we were gone before she could open her eyes.

She couldn't know we'd been there. If she did, we'd have to explain what was going on. And there was no way to do that without revealing Zane's secret.

"Are you sure she had enough?" I asked Zane as we hurried back to the water dorm.

"I'm sure."

I accepted his answer, and we made our way back in silence.

Alyssa was going to be confused when she woke up, especially because the infirmary was deserted, and everyone was asleep. But she'd be healed and awake, and that was all that mattered.

Once back in Zane's room, I wrapped my arms around myself awkwardly, unsure what to do next. We had a few hours to kill, and we had to stay put, so people could see me leaving his room.

"Are you tired?" he asked. "Do you want to go back to sleep?"

"No." I shrugged, and then I added, "I don't need a lot of sleep."

"Oh," he said, surprising me by not asking more about it. Not like I would have had any answers. "Want to watch tv?"

I should have said no. There were so many more productive ways we could use this time—mainly, I could ask him questions to get as much information about the immortals and the Norse gods as possible.

But while my body wasn't tired, my mind was exhausted. So much had happened over the past few days, and I needed an escape from it all, even if that escape only lasted a few hours.

"Sure," I said, and we situated ourselves on his couch, and settled in to watch the first show recommended on his Netflix account.

We sat close, but not so close that we were touching, and watched for a few hours. The crackle of tension between us kept making me want to move closer, but I miraculously resisted. From the way he remained focused on the tv and didn't look over at me, I had a feeling he was going through the same struggle.

Eventually, we heard movement in the halls.

It didn't take long for my phone to start ringing like crazy.

Nicole.

I picked it up after a few rings.

"Hello?" I made sure I sounded groggy—like I was waking up after a terrible hangover.

"Come to the infirmary—now." She somehow didn't sound tired at all. "Alyssa's awake."

CHAPTER TWENTY-SEVEN

"I still can't believe my parents tried to bring me home when I was like that."

Alyssa was sitting on the couch in her room, drinking a glass of red wine as if she hadn't been barely clinging to life less than twenty-four hours ago.

Just like Zane had promised, she was one hundred percent healed.

I'd spent the past few hours filling her in on everything that had happened while she'd been in her coma. At least, I filled her in on all the *official* stuff that had happened. There was so much I couldn't say, but I'd been getting good at skirting around the truth nowadays.

"They should be here in about an hour," she continued, since the first thing her parents had done when they learned about Alyssa's recovery was hop on the first flight from Boston to DC. They'd be staying on campus—the academy had a small hotel for visitors.

They believed Hecate was responsible for Alyssa's miracle recovery.

They'd probably have heart attacks if they knew the truth.

"I can't believe I missed Greek Week," she kept talking, oblivious to the fact that I was barely chiming into the conversation. She needed to talk, so I'd let her talk. It was easier for me that way. "Especially the ball. It sounds like it got wild."

"You have no idea," I said, flashing back to everything that had happened last night.

Vera coming at me with murder in her eyes.

Plunging my dagger into her heart.

Hiding her body in the frozen lake.

Those images were going to be seared in my mind forever.

"And I can't believe you slept at Zane's *again* without hooking up."

"We were both pretty drunk," I repeated the story we were going with. "We passed out immediately after we got back."

"So are the two of you a thing now?"

"I don't know what we are." I shrugged, wanting to get away from the topic of Zane as quickly as possible.

She frowned and took a sip of her wine.

My watch buzzed, and I glanced down at it.

A text from Kate.

Come to the cottage. Now.

My heart stopped.

She knew. Somehow, she knew. I had no idea how she could have found out, but this was it. The secrets had finally caught up to me.

My body felt as cold as the lake we'd dropped Vera into last night.

"You okay?" Alyssa asked.

"Yeah," I lied. "Totally fine."

"Who was that?" She glanced at my watch.

"Kate." I stood, too restless to remain sitting. "I have to go."

"Why's Kate texting you?"

I pressed my lips together, realizing too late that it would be strange to get a casual text from the headmistress. I should have lied about who it was.

"No idea," I said. "Maybe she wants to talk to the champions of each dorm?"

"Maybe," she said. "You should go. Jamie's been blowing up my phone—I'm gonna go hang out with her for a bit."

"Good idea," I said. "She's been a wreck since the attack."

I told her I'd see her later, then went back into my room to bundle up.

At least, I hoped I'd see her later. If Kate had any idea of what I'd truly been up to last night, I had no idea what she'd do with me.

Hopefully she wouldn't throw me in that dungeon.

My lungs tightened at the thought, like I was suffocating.

It probably has nothing to do with last night, I thought, trying to talk myself down as I made my way to the cottage. Because it could have to do with my metal magic, or Hades being my father, or maybe she'd gotten news from my mom. She, Nicole, and Blake had been keeping me in the loop about everything so far. They'd been treating me like I was one of them—an original Elemental. Besides, if they had any inclination about what had truly happened last night, they'd probably burst into my room guns blazing—not politely request me to meet them in the cottage.

It's fine, I thought, taking a deep breath of the icy air. *Everything's going to be fine.*

My cheeks felt frozen as I made my way up the porch steps of the cottage.

There was no turning back now. Anyway, where would I go if I did?

I knocked, the door opened... and Mason stood on the other side, looking as arrogant as ever.

I wanted to turn on my heel and run. But my feet were frozen in place.

"Summer," he said with a broad, knowing smile. "How nice of you to join us."

"What are you doing here?" I asked.

"Having a meeting." He stepped aside so I could enter. "Why don't you come in?"

I swallowed and stepped inside, searching his eyes for a hint of what might be going on, but found nothing.

Kate, Nicole, Blake, and Zane were all gathered in the living room.

My head felt fuzzy, and I braced myself for anything, vaguely aware of the door clicking shut behind me and trapping me inside.

I focused on Zane, wishing our soulmate bond came with telepathy. Because what was he doing here? As far as Nicole, Blake, and Kate knew, Zane was as clueless as any other student in the school about the Norse gods. And as far as the others knew, Zane was also clueless about the fact that my element was metal and not air.

"Mason figured out the truth," Blake said quickly.

"Really?" I said, since there were so many truths he could be referring to.

"I knew there was something different about your magic." Mason eyed me as if telling me to stay quiet—he had it handled. "I was close to piecing it together, especially after the tournament this week. Then I heard you telling Zane everything last night at the ball that your affinity isn't air. It's metal. You're a daughter of Hades. The only daughter of Hades, if what we know about history is correct. The moment I heard that, it all clicked into place."

All right. I could roll with that lie.

If that was what had truly happened, what would I do right now?

I'd feel ashamed of myself for telling Zane my secret while I'd been drunk.

I turned to Kate, and it wasn't hard to replace my fear with shame, since that was an emotion I'd become accustomed to recently. "I'm so sorry," I said. "I must have had too much champagne. I barely remember what happened…"

Tears welled in my eyes—real tears. I felt so guilty about all these lies that it was going to flow out of me.

"The champagne was tampered with," Kate said, and my stomach flipped so much that I almost fell over.

"What?" I said, trying to steady myself. "How…"

I wanted to ask how she knew, but I let the sentence trail from there.

"We suspect the Norse intercepted it at some point," Blake said. "And that they put something in it."

"Mead," Kate supplied. "I've researched enough to know that mead is a powerful drink of the Norse gods. Given what happened last night, I gather it's far more potent for those without Norse heritage."

Wow—she'd put that together quickly. She was clearly making a lot of headway on her research.

"Why would they do that?" I asked, remembering to play clueless.

Fire blazed in Blake's eyes. "One of them got past our barrier," he said. "They broke into our holding cell and escaped with the handmaiden we were keeping there."

"Wow." I figured the fewer words I said, the better.

"It gets worse," Kate said gently, and she took a deep breath, looking like she was preparing to deliver bad news. "Vera went on a walk to get some air after seeing you with Zane. Mason saw her leave through the back."

I glanced at Mason, who nodded, confirming Kate's words.

"I followed Vera to see what was wrong, and tried to get her to stay." He had the gall to glance down at his feet, as though he was ashamed. "Her emotions were probably heightened by the mead. She pushed past me and said she was going for a walk. I let her leave."

"It wasn't your fault," Kate said firmly. "There was no reason to think the academy grounds weren't safe."

"*What* wasn't his fault?" I asked, remembering I was supposed to be clueless about what had happened to Vera.

"We believe that Fulla—the handmaiden we were keeping here—took Vera," Blake said. "It seems like Vera went for a walk around the lake—"

"She did that whenever she was upset," Zane interjected.

My stomach twisted so much with all these lies that I couldn't bring myself to look at him or Mason.

"The place where we were keeping Fulla was near the lake," Blake continued. "We found some pieces of Vera's dress on the ground nearby. It seems like Fulla and whoever helped her escape fought with Vera and took her with them."

"They *took her?*" I repeated, dazed.

I'd been bracing myself for them to tell me that Vera was dead.

This was unexpected.

"We held Fulla captive. It makes sense that she'd want to do the same with one of us. But it was no one's fault," he said, glancing at Mason. "Vera was drunk, and at the wrong place at the wrong time."

"How do you know she was taken?" I asked. "How do you know she isn't…"

Dead.

I couldn't speak the word.

"There was no blood, and no body," Blake said calmly. "We searched the surrounding area. Every piece of evidence points to Vera being taken. And we expect she's still alive, because if Fulla wanted her dead, she easily could have done it at the lake."

I glanced at Zane.

His eyes were as hollow as they'd been last night when we lowered Vera's body into the water.

"She's out there," Nicole said firmly. "And we're going to do everything possible to get her back."

"No," Kate said, and I looked at her, shocked. *"I'm* going to do everything possible, by researching to figure out where Fulla may have taken her. Because right now, the five of you have something else you need to do."

CHAPTER TWENTY-EIGHT

"What do we need to do?" I stiffened, caught off-guard.

"As you know, we've been questioning Fulla," Blake said, and I nodded for him to continue. "We learned that the handmaidens infiltrated the academy because they were after some of the weapons we keep here."

"My bow and arrows, which were gifted to me by my father, and can hit any visible target," Nicole said. "And the Golden Sword of Athena, which can cut through anything, no matter how strong the material."

"They wanted the arrows and sword to help them find one of their own weapons," Blake continued. He and Nicole were insanely in sync when they spoke, effortlessly playing off each other. "Thor's Hammer has been taken by the immortals. They've buried it in the highest peak of their home in the Appalachian Mountains—"

"Wait," I said, since I was supposed to be clueless about all of this. "Who are the immortals?"

Again, I couldn't bring myself to look at Zane or Mason. I was afraid that if I did, I'd give myself away.

Give *all* of us away.

"Sorry—Blake got ahead of himself," Kate said, and then she explained the basics of the immortals. It was information I'd already learned from Zane, but I asked questions as if I was hearing it all for the first time. "Fulla barely told us anything about the Norse gods, but she had no qualms giving us information about the immortals," she continued. "The immortals and the Norse gods don't like each other very much."

"Definitely," Blake said. "But the point here is that Thor's Hammer is one of the most powerful Norse weapons. We do *not* want to go up against Thor if he has his hammer. So now that we know its location, we need to get it before the Norse gods can steal it back from the immortals. We were going to get more information out of Fulla before leaving on the mission, but now that she's gone, there's no better time to head out than the present."

"And you want us to help you." I had a hard time believing it, given that they had years of experience on us.

Well, they had years of experience on *me*. Zane was another matter entirely. But they didn't know about that.

"Thor's Hammer is made of metal," Nicole said. "Given that your affinity is metal, we think you'd be a huge asset to the quest. Plus, we know your true potential."

"Meaning that we know you let Topher win in your face off," Kate said. "You were smart in doing so."

"You let him win?" Zane looked honestly confused.

"It's a long story," I said. "But yes."

"Was it because you didn't want to fight me?"

"No." I rolled my eyes. "Trust me—I would have loved to fight you."

"Good." He smiled wickedly. "I would hate to think you'd turn down a challenge."

His comment lit a flame inside me, but instead of feeding into it, I acted annoyed and turned back to Nicole. "And you're inviting Zane because…?"

"Firstly, because he's the Greek Week champion," she said. "His skills were impressive—he's better than most of the teachers at this school. You two were able to defeat that handmaiden in the woods by yourselves, which was highly impressive. Secondly—and most importantly—because he's the only person at the academy other than us who knows the truth about your magic. It would overly complicate things if you had to hide your abilities on this quest."

"It's the most logical choice," Kate added.

"Got it," I said, feeling a rush of relief at the idea of getting out of the academy for a bit. Then again, it was for an actual quest that could get us killed. Reminding myself of that made the relief vanish in an instant. "When do we leave?"

"Tomorrow morning," she said. "But first, I have something for you."

She walked upstairs, then came back holding a sword.

A *golden* sword.

The power radiating off it was stronger than any I'd felt from a metal weapon. It was like a siren's song pulling me closer. Suddenly, I was in front of Kate, my hands reaching for the sword, hungry to touch it.

She stepped back, and I snapped out of my trance. "I've been keeping a secret," she started. "The god of darkness, Erebus, stopped by to return this sword to me a few weeks ago. He didn't say why, but I figured I'd eventually figure it out. Now, I can't think of anyone on this planet more worthy of handling the Golden Sword of Athena than you. But I'll hand it over when we meet back here tomorrow morning. For now, you all need to get some rest. We have a big day coming up, and you need to be ready for it."

Especially Alyssa. I finally got her back, and now I was about to leave.

Who knew when—or if—we'd be back.

Don't think like that, I reminded myself. *Zane and Mason are immortals. If anyone can keep us safe in their mountains, it's them.*

Assuming they wanted to keep us safe. What if this

was a big plan of Mason's, so the immortals could capture Nicole and Blake? Or worse—kill them? And while I wanted to think Zane was on our side, I knew better than to assume anything with him. He said he'd do anything to protect me, and I believed him. But he saw Nicole and Blake as the enemy. There was no knowing what he'd do to them.

"We'll say it has to do with Greek Week," Kate said simply. "There are many other covens around the world. After Zane's incredible displays of power, it would be natural for their leaders to want to meet him. And, if given the option to bring someone with him, I think it's clear after last night that he'd choose you."

I inwardly groaned at the reminder that everyone at the school was probably talking about me going back to Zane's room last night.

Maybe it would be good to get out of here for a bit. Especially because I didn't think I could look at that lake without feeling sick about what had happened with Vera.

But despite my own desires, none of this was worth Nicole and Blake's lives.

"Maybe we should wait," I said. "Learn more about the mountains and the hammer before heading out."

"If you don't want to come, it's okay." Nicole gave me an understanding smile. "We know it's a lot to ask, given that you only just learned about your magic a few weeks ago."

Except I knew enough about the story of the original Elementals to know they'd faced quests like this soon after receiving their elemental magic. If they could do it, so could I. And I could tell from the confidence in Nicole's expression that she felt the same.

"But we need to get that hammer before Thor," Blake added. "We're leaving tomorrow, no matter what."

Crap.

This meant I *had* to go. If I didn't, that meant one less person on Nicole and Blake's side. And despite my connection with Zane, I *was* on their side.

Somehow, I needed to keep all three of them safe.

As for Mason... I wasn't exactly having warm and fuzzy feelings about him right now. Not that I ever did, but if he tried to harm them, I'd have no issues doing whatever was necessary to keep them safe.

And while immortals were strong, I doubted any of them would want to go up against the Golden Sword of Athena. Especially with me wielding it.

"No." I forced confidence into my tone. "I'm coming with you. Because even though I'm new here, I can help you."

"That's the spirit." Nicole smiled again, more genuinely this time. "And clearly, we feel the same. You wouldn't be here right now otherwise."

"So, I'll see you all here tomorrow morning?" Kate asked.

"Only if you promise you're actually giving me that sword," I joked, trying to lighten the mood.

It came out half-heartedly. I'd never been one who excelled at lightening the mood. It was probably that whole "daughter of the god of the Underworld" thing I had going for me.

"I'm *loaning* you the sword," Kate said. "But like I said earlier, it's time for you to get some rest. You're going to need it for the quest tomorrow."

With that, we all said goodnight, and I left with Zane and Mason, the three of us eventually splitting ways to head back to our dorms. I wasn't sure I'd be able to rest, but I needed to try.

Because Kate was right—I'd need it to be at my full strength for whatever we'd be facing tomorrow.

CHAPTER TWENTY-NINE

I was halfway back to the air dorm when someone came up from behind me and grabbed my hand.

Zane.

He was like a marble statue in the cold, dark night.

I watched him and waited, not pulling away.

"We need to talk," he said, and he led me off the path and into the shadows behind one of the academic buildings, where no one else would be able to hear or see us.

Not like there were many people walking around campus, since they all had pretty nasty hangovers after the incident with the mead last night.

"I know you're hesitant about this quest," he started.

I pulled my hand out of his and crossed my arms. "What makes you think that? The fact that we're going into the Immortal Mountains with two people you and Mason consider enemies? And that Nicole and Blake are clueless about how much danger they're truly walking into?"

"I'm going to keep you safe," he promised. "*All* of you."

"Including Nicole and Blake?"

"Yes."

I was caught so off-guard that I could barely breathe. "Why would you want to do that?"

"Remember what I told you, about how the immortals aren't on the side of either the Greeks or the Norse?"

"How could I forget?"

He ignored my sarcasm and continued, "We want the Greeks and Norse to fight each other, so both sides will weaken. If we steal the hammer and bring it back here, you can bet Thor and his siblings aren't going to let that slide."

"They'll attack the academy."

"Yes."

"So we shouldn't go at all," I said quickly. "We should make something up to tell Kate—something that will make her want to leave the hammer where it is."

"And then the Norse gods will go up the mountains, get the hammer, and be stronger when the war starts with them and the Greeks," he said.

"You're saying it's a lose-lose."

"The immortals are the ones who are going to come

out on top," he said, as if it were a fact I should already know.

"So your answer to my question is yes."

He simply shrugged. "Kate, Nicole, and Blake know the Norse are going to be angry after we retrieve the hammer," he said. "They know what they're getting into. But as they just told us, they've decided it's better to risk the Norse being angry at them than to eventually go against Thor and his hammer. There's nothing you can say to change their mind about this quest."

"I could tell them the truth." I narrowed my eyes in challenge.

He didn't appear the slightest bit worried that I'd follow through on the threat. "If you do that, they'll still want that hammer," he said. "The only difference will be that Mason and I will be dead—or locked in that torture chamber of theirs—and they'll lose any trust they had in you."

As they should, I thought, although I didn't say it out loud.

The unfortunate fact here was that all of Zane's points were solid. War *was* coming, and we'd be better with the hammer than without it.

The fact that we were facing an actual war with Norse gods still didn't feel real to me. It was like I was living someone else's life, and that I could wake up any day and have everything go back to the way it was before I unleashed my magic on Courtney, was attacked by a harpy, and was whisked away to the academy.

But this was real. And I needed to do everything I could to keep myself and my friends alive.

And Zane, that annoying voice in the back of my head reminded me.

Not like Zane would ever need my help. He'd more than proven that he could take care of himself.

"It's in my best interest to keep Blake and Nicole safe," he continued. "I know how to avoid running into any other immortals while we make our way up to the location where the hammer is buried. They won't even know we're there. And I'll do everything in my power to ensure that the five of us return safely to the academy with the hammer in hand."

From the determination in his eyes, I could tell he meant it.

"Not so fast," a familiar voice said, and Mason stepped out of the shadows.

My heart jumped. "How long have you been there?"

"A while." He smiled slowly and prowled toward us. "I excel at hiding in the shadows."

A shiver ran up my spine at the conniving way he spoke. Because gone was the joking, smirking teacher I'd known for the past few weeks. A cold, strategic immortal now stood in his place.

"I'm afraid I can't make the same promise as your soulmate just did," he continued before I could reply.

Zane stiffened and studied Mason, his hands clenched by his sides. "Helping the Greeks complete this mission is our best move," he said. "You should know that."

"Giving me the hammer after we retrieve it is our best move," he said simply. "Consider it the favor you owe me for helping you cover up the murders you committed."

"Why do you want the hammer so badly?" I asked.

Zane kept his gaze locked on Mason's and said nothing, seemingly backing up my question.

"Because we have no idea what's going to happen after we dig up the hammer," Mason said. "It will be in the best hands with an older, more experienced immortal."

He stared Zane down, making the pecking order between them clear.

Suspicion stirred inside me. "I'm the one with metal magic," I said to Mason. "I should bring the hammer down the mountain."

"You'll already have the Golden Sword," Zane said. "And I do see Mason's point. It's best that one of us ensures that the hammer is safely brought to the academy than one of them."

I hated the way he said one of *us*.

He truly believed I was on his and Mason's side.

"Why do you assume Nicole or Blake won't want to

carry the hammer back to the school?" I asked. "They're the ones in charge of this mission."

"Leave that up to me," Mason said. "As long as you give me the hammer, I'll keep Nicole and Blake alive. If not..." He trailed off, the threat lingering in the air.

"You'd really kill them for bringing the hammer back to the school instead of you?" I asked, since it seemed so unimportant in the scheme of things.

"Yes." From the intensity in his eyes, I knew he was telling the truth.

He must really not trust Nicole and Blake with that hammer.

He clearly didn't trust me with it, either.

"But if you kill them, Kate will think the immortals were responsible for their deaths," I pointed out. "Which is exactly what you don't want, since you want the immortals to stay on the sidelines during this war."

"She makes a good point." Zane stood shoulder to shoulder with me, so it felt like the two of us against Mason.

"You say that as if I haven't already thought it through." Mason shook his head at us like we were children. Which, given how much older he likely was than us, we probably were. "I'd tell Kate that the Norse found us on the mountains and fought us for the hammer, and that Nicole and Blake were casualties of the attack. It'll fire up the Greeks even more to make the first move against the Norse. Now that I think about it..."

"Fine," I said before he could continue, holding up a hand to signal him to stop talking. "I'll let you bring the hammer down the mountain. In return, you make sure Nicole and Blake make it back with us to the academy *unharmed.*"

I didn't have much bargaining power here, since I was the one who owed Mason the favor, but I still needed to try.

"Deal," he said, and I relaxed, but not much. Because I had no way to make sure he kept his word. I just didn't know what else there was to do, especially since the important thing was that the hammer made it back to the academy. It didn't actually matter which of us brought it down.

Anyway, I'd have the Golden Sword of Athena. From the moment I'd laid sight on the sword, I knew it was mine. More so than Thor's Hammer could ever be.

"A good decision," Zane said to Mason. "Nicole and Blake are strong players. It will be interesting to see how they fare against the Norse once they go up against each other."

He said it so coldly, like they were pawns in a game designed for the entertainment of the immortals. Like it didn't matter to him if they lived or died.

The only reason he cared about keeping them alive

right now was because of his promise to me. Which, I supposed, did mean something. Plus, purposefully sounding this cold when he spoke to Mason could be part of how he was watching out for them.

I had to believe that. Because Zane had a soul. He—and all the immortals—wouldn't have soulmates if they didn't.

"Anyway." Mason smiled, clearly feeling like he'd won. "We should go to bed. We have a long few days ahead of us."

Zane turned his focus to me. "Do you want me to walk you back?" he asked, ignoring Mason.

"No," I said, since after hearing how cold he'd sounded while speaking about Nicole and Blake, I trusted him even less than I had before. "I can get there myself."

Not in the mood to talk about it further, I turned around and headed back to the air dorm, unsure how I'd possibly get any sleep given what we were about to do tomorrow.

CHAPTER THIRTY

I barely slept that night. Between all my tossing and turning, my Apple Watch reported that I'd gotten about two hours in. Which would be far more bearable for me than it would be for someone who needed a full night's sleep, but I ended up falling asleep in the back of the car ride to the mountains—and waking up snuggled into Zane's side, my head resting on his chest.

The moment I woke up, I sat ramrod straight, refusing to look at him. Instead, I stared straight ahead, since Mason was on my other side and I didn't want to look at him, either.

Lots of girls would be thrilled to be crammed in the middle seat of the back of a car, squished between two gorgeous immortal men.

Me, not so much.

Although it was impossible to deny the way my skin

tingled at every place it touched Zane's. Which was basically everywhere from the bottom of my legs to my shoulder.

Blake was at the wheel, driving us along narrow roads that wound around the massive, snow-covered mountains. It was like we'd entered an enchanted ice realm.

Which we sort of had, since these mountains were the homes of the immortals.

Then a semi-truck came around the bend ahead and drove past us, shattering the illusion.

"How far are we?" I rubbed at my eyes, as if that could help me wake up.

"Coffee?" Nicole asked from the passenger side, reaching down for the thermos at her feet and filling me a paper cup before I could answer. She held it up near Blake. "Warm it up."

He took one hand off the wheel and wrapped it around the cup. Orange magic glowed from his palm, and steam rose out of the cup.

"Perfect," Nicole said.

Blake placed his hand back on the wheel, and Nicole twisted around to hand the cup to me.

"Thanks." I took it from her and blew on the steaming hot liquid, even though I'd never acquired a taste for coffee. My mom preferred tea—she had an entire cabinet dedicated to different varieties of it—so that was what I'd grown up drinking.

"We're almost there," Zane answered my question. "We entered the Appalachians a while back."

"In West Virginia," Blake said. "A state I never imagined I'd end up visiting."

"You and me both," I said, since while I'd always wanted to see the country beyond Florida, West Virginia hadn't been on my bucket list.

I sipped the coffee as we drove in silence—we must have been so far out that there wasn't any signal to play music. Nicole had a map on her lap, our route highlighted, and she told Blake whenever we had to turn. The roads were narrower now—too narrow for any semitrucks to drive through—and ice crystals hung from the bare branches of the trees towering around us. Unlike the main roads through the mountains, this one hadn't been plowed, but the SUV was equipped to handle the snow and ice.

"The temperature's dropping fast," Blake eventually said. "Almost ten degrees in the past five minutes."

"Just what Fulla said would happen when we got closer." Nicole peered out the window, then pointed to an even smaller road. "There."

Blake turned, and the road quickly ended at a snow-covered clearing next to the forest. All that remained was a path leading into the trees, which was too narrow for the car to enter.

"This is it," Nicole said. "The start of the trail up the Immortal Mountains."

"We walk from here," Blake said. "We're far enough off the road that no one's going to see the car."

"What about the tracks?" I asked, but when I turned around to look out the back window, they were gone.

Magic tingled along my arms.

The path ahead wasn't what would lead us to the Immortal Mountains. Because we'd already *entered* the Immortal Mountains.

Mason opened the door, and I was immediately assaulted by blisteringly cold air. I sucked in a sharp breath, and it stung my lungs, making me feel like I was freezing from the inside-out.

"I'll get the stuff from the back," Mason said. "Because we're definitely going to need to bundle up."

Thirty minutes later, we were all wearing the winter gear Kate had the foresight to pack for us. There were layers of it, and I was exhausted simply from getting dressed. But the clothes brought the cold from assaultingly painful to terribly miserable, which I was grateful for.

Blake handed us our packs, and Nicole helped me fasten a belt around my waist so I could sheath the Golden Sword.

Once situated, we faced the start of the trail. The tree branches curved into an arch overhead, making it look like a door to an evil realm. It looked darker inside there, too.

"I hope this isn't like the Whispering Forest in Kerberos," Nicole said in a low, cautious voice.

"I'm sure it's going to be fine," Blake said. "After making it through the Whispering Forest, we can make it through anything."

"What's the Whispering Forest?" I asked.

"A place you never want to go," Nicole said, her eyes dark and hollow. "A place that sucks you into your darkest fears, until you get so lost in its maze that you can't find your way out."

"The immortals are powerful, but they can't manipulate Earth in that sort of way," Mason said confidently. "Fulla would have warned us if they could."

"You're giving her a lot of trust," Blake said, marching toward the forest. "But let's go. The longer we stand here staring, the less territory we can cover before nightfall."

He stepped through the arch with what seemed like no fear in the world.

"How is it?" Nicole asked.

"All good," Blake said.

Nicole followed, then Mason.

The three of them faced Zane and me, waiting.

"You go first." Zane motioned to the entrance. "I'll be right behind you."

Nicole nodded encouragingly.

So I took a deep breath of freezing air and walked toward the arch, the snow crunching under my boots as I forged my own path. I glanced up at the ice-covered branches, then stepped under them to join Nicole, Blake, and Mason on the other side.

Like Blake had told us, nothing felt different. No electric buzz through my body, and no more sudden decreases in temperature. It was so alarmingly *normal.*

Well, as normal as things could get in mystical mountains.

Zane stepped through the arch and automatically moved to my side.

"All good?" he asked me.

"All good," I confirmed, and then the group of us spun around to face the ghostly forest and started on our way.

CHAPTER THIRTY-ONE

We walked for hours. It was darker in the forest, like the sun was constantly trying to set but getting nowhere. None of us said much—we were conserving energy to walk as far as possible by nightfall.

Suddenly, something crunched in the trees ahead.

Blake stopped and held his hands up in the universal signal to stay still and keep quiet. He met all our eyes, making sure we understood.

I breathed as slowly and steadily as possible, trying to be as still as the icy trees surrounding us.

Nicole reached for the bow strapped behind her back —somehow not making any noise—and strung an arrow through it, standing at the ready.

I slowly reached for the handle of the Golden Sword, preparing myself in case I had to quickly unsheathe it.

The metal hummed in my hand, connecting with the magic running inside my veins.

The others held their hands steadily in front of themselves, ready to use their magic if needed.

Zane and Mason had promised they knew how to avoid the immortals. But what if they were wrong? As far as I knew, they hadn't been here since the second semester at the academy had started. Things could have changed since then.

Or else... what other creatures resided in the forest?

Flashes of the troll Alyssa and I had fought in the alley crossed my mind, and dread rushed through me. But if it were a troll, then we were five against one. We'd be able to easily take it down.

Unless it was a *pack* of trolls.

I blinked and snapped myself out of it, reminding myself of an important thing Mason had taught us in class. Stay present. Don't worry about what you *might* face. Focus on what you *are* facing. The second you get lost in your mind is the second you might end up dead.

The steps moved closer and closer... and a goat ambled out of the thicket of trees.

Nicole smirked and released an arrow.

Blake stayed where he was, keeping his hands up to tell us to remain quiet.

We remained frozen like that for what felt like an hour, although it was probably only a few minutes.

No more noises sounded from the trees.

"I think we're in the clear," Blake said, although he spoke quietly, just in case.

"Perfect." Nicole marched toward the goat and plucked the arrow out of its chest, placing it back into her quiver. "And this couldn't have come at a better time. Because I *really* wasn't looking forward to forcing down those dehydrated meal packs we brought for dinner."

I had zero wilderness survival skills, but the others were able to gather what we needed to start a fire. I liked to think the few sticks I found helped, but they definitely could have gotten it done without my help.

Blake started the fire, using his magic to extend the heat outward, and I relished in thawing my extremities.

Nicole and Mason got to work on preparing the goat for us to eat, and while I'd never considered going vegetarian, the thought definitely crossed my mind after seeing a goat skinned and drained. I had to turn my head, trying my best to stay occupied on removing the plates and silverware from our packs and readying them so we could eat.

Once the food was ready, we devoured the meat in silence. Both Zane and Mason wolfed it down, like it was the most delicious meal on the planet. They must have eaten double the amount of Blake.

I supposed immortals needed more food than the rest of us witches and demigods.

Despite how much they ate, there was still a *lot* leftover. So Zane and Blake did something with their magic to dry it out like jerky, so we'd be able to continue to eat it on our journey.

I wanted to remain by the fire, dreading the trek through the cold. But we had a mission to accomplish, so eventually we packed up and continued our hike.

We walked mostly in silence—our energy needed to be saved for the journey. Even the energy expended in conversation mattered.

After a few hours, the sun started setting, and the temperature felt like it had dropped twenty degrees. Despite every inch of my body being covered, the cold was soaking into my bones.

Suddenly, Blake stopped walking, staring ahead.

One by one, we joined him and faced where he was looking—a cave. It was about double Mason's height, and looked like a dark, gaping mouth waiting to devour us whole.

Shivers crawled down my spine.

"Looks like we found our shelter for the night," Nicole declared.

"Assuming nothing else is already occupying it," I said.

"Too bad." She shrugged and reached for her bow. "They won't be occupying it for long."

Blake smirked and created a small fireball in his hand.

It was official—they were crazy. It seemed like they actually *liked* facing down monsters and killing them.

"Are you sure that's a good idea?" I asked, unease continuing to creep up on me. "I thought we brought a tent and sleeping rolls for a reason." I glanced at Blake's giant pack, where the said items were being kept.

"The cave will be safer than a tent," Zane said. "We'll have only one place to worry about protecting, instead of an entire perimeter."

I sighed, knowing I'd been outvoted. Especially because Zane had promised to keep us safe.

If he thought goading a potential monster and sleeping in a cave was the best option for the night, then fine.

At least I had the Golden Sword of Athena. I could slice this cave monster no matter what it was made of. I reached for its handle, and the metal warmed, reminding me it was there for me.

Nicole pulled an arrow out of her quiver, strung it through her bow, and looked to Blake. "Light me up," she said with a mischievous grin.

"You got it." He tossed a fireball toward her, lighting

up the tip of her arrow, and she sent it soaring into the cave. It went so far that the light from the fire disappeared into the darkness.

They did this again and again, sending countless arrows inside. Her quiver was never-ending, as if it refilled on its own.

It probably *did* refill on its own.

I kept my sword at the ready, prepared to take down whatever came out of there. Mason did the same, as did Zane with his dagger.

A low, painful groan sounded from inside the cave.

Nicole kept her current flaming arrow strung through the bow, her gray eyes narrowed as she focused on the cave.

The groans got closer—a chorus of them.

My breathing shallowed, and the sword's magic flowed through me, every muscle in my body ready to strike.

Shadows moved closer in the darkness, walking slowly toward us, sounding like they were dragging their feet. But they weren't just shadows. They were eyes.

Glowing blue, inhuman eyes. Ten or more pairs of them.

And they were all focused on us.

Nicole let her arrow fly.

It struck right below the closest one's head, into its chest where its heart should be, lighting up its face.

No—not its face.

Its *skull*.

That thing was a walking skeleton.

The creature flinched back, and the fire went out. But it kept dragging forward, as if nothing had happened.

Nicole sent more arrows flying, lighting up the cave so we could get a better look at what we were dealing with.

Skeletons—all of them. Ambling toward us like zombies.

"My arrows aren't doing anything," Nicole stated the obvious.

"That's because those are draugr," Zane said. "There's only one way to kill them—decapitation."

Blake removed his sword from its sheath. "Then let's decapitate these bad boys," he said, and he rushed toward them, ready to strike.

More magic from the Golden Sword rushed through me, and I ran toward the zombie-skeletons, ready to take them down. In my peripheral vision, I saw the others do the same.

I hurried toward the first one, focused on its hideous, glowing eyes, and it was like the sword was a living thing in my hands as I sliced through the bones in the monster's neck.

The skeleton disintegrated into ash, and I sucked in a sharp breath, gazing at the sword in shock.

"Summer!" Nicole screamed. "Behind you!"

I spun around and faced another skeleton, its hands outstretched so its fingers were inches away from grabbing my shoulders. Its mouth was open, ready to bite me.

I decapitated it before it could.

It was a humble reminder that while the sword was strong and gave me more power, it wouldn't fight for me. I had to remain aware, like I'd been taught in training.

At some point, Zane made his way to my side. We stood with our backs to each other and fought against the skeletons together, as if we'd trained like this. We moved in tandem, our bodies keeping time with each other in a perfectly choreographed dance. Together, we were unstoppable.

After about five minutes, all the skeletons had been turned to ash.

They might have been creepy-looking, but they had nothing on us.

Even though they were all dead, Zane and I kept our backs pressed against each other, our breathing slowing at the same pace.

Mason sheathed his sword and examined the piles of ashes on the ground. "Good job," he said, as if he was teaching a class instead of fighting in real life.

Zane and I separated, so we both faced the cave. I didn't look at him, but the energy humming between our bodies was more intense than ever. It was like we were made to fight together.

Nicole kept an arrow pointed steadily at the mouth of the cave. "Are you sure that's all of them?" She glanced at Zane, as if he'd know the answer simply because he knew what the creatures were called.

"There's only one way to find out," Blake said. "Mason—come into the cave with me to see what's in there. The three of you, stay out here and keep watch."

"Going into the cave is more dangerous than keeping watch," Zane said. "I'll keep Summer safe out here. Nicole, you go with them."

"The two of you might be excellent fighters, but you're still students," she said. "No matter how talented and gifted you are, the three of us have years of training on you. We're not leaving you out here alone."

I gazed into the dark, gaping mouth of the cave, still not wanting to go inside.

"Zane, come with us," Blake said before either of us could speak. "Nicole's bow and arrow and Summer's Golden Sword will be more than enough to defend against anything that might attack out here."

Zane looked to me, as if asking my permission.

In what universe did Zane ask my permission for *anything*?

"Blake's right," I said. "Nicole and I've got this. The three of you can handle whatever's in there."

Especially since two of the three of you are immortals, I thought.

No one said a word.

I squelched away whatever minor part of me wanted to volunteer to go in Zane's place. Because not only was he more experienced than I was—especially since these were Norse monsters—but there was also a part of me that didn't want to leave him alone with Nicole.

He'd promised he wouldn't hurt her, and I believed him. But I didn't want to test it out.

"The two of you will be fine out here," Zane said. "Once we know the caves are clear, we'll come back to get you, and then we can take shelter for the night."

He sounded so confident, and I knew he wouldn't tell us this if he didn't think we'd be safe. He knew these mountains. We'd be fine.

"Good luck," I said, even though he didn't need any, and he hurried with the other guys to venture inside the cave.

CHAPTER THIRTY-TWO

"Zane knew what those monsters were pretty quickly," Nicole observed once the guys were gone.

"He's interested in mythology—all types of it," I immediately jumped to his defense. "He has books about the mythologies of tons of cultures in his room."

She smirked when I mentioned his room, and my cheeks heated as I waited for her to ask me what had happened between us.

At least it would distract from his obvious knowledge of Norse mythology.

"The two of you fought really well together," she said instead. "It was impressive."

"Thanks." I was unsure if I was thanking her for the compliment, or for not prying into my personal life.

It was probably a bit of both.

"What are you going to do with the hammer after we get it to the academy?" I asked, wanting to bring the conversation away from Zane.

"Keep it away from Thor," she said simply. "I'm sure Kate is coming up with a way to do that as we speak."

"You really trust her, don't you?" I asked.

"With my life."

It wasn't long before Mason emerged from the cave to let us know there hadn't been any more monsters inside.

"Nicole—help me collect some firewood," he said. "Summer—go in the cave and help them get settled in."

I stiffened at the thought of Mason out here alone with Nicole. If something "mysteriously" happened to her, there were all sort of things he could blame it on…

"I'll help you guys," I said, marching into the forest without leaving any room for debate.

Mason scowled, but said nothing.

Nicole made idle conversation as we chose the best pieces of wood, but the tension between me and Mason was palpable in the freezing air. So she stayed by my side, as if she could tell there was something going on between me and Mason and wanted to protect me.

If she asked, what should I say?

Maybe that he was upset I'd lost the first battle round in Greek Week. After all, he'd seen how well I'd just fought with Zane. Surely he was wondering why I hadn't brought that to the competition.

It might make sense. Sort of.

I remained lost in thought as we finished gathering the wood. Sure, it was awkward, but I didn't know what Mason would have done if I'd left him alone with Nicole, and I was glad I wasn't going to find out.

Once we'd gathered enough firewood, we ventured into the cave. It was nearly pitch dark, minus the flicker of fire in the distance. A draft passed through the air, and I felt like I was walking into the Underworld.

I hugged the firewood to my chest, finding comfort at the solidness of it, as if it could protect me.

But protect me from *what?* The others wouldn't have told us to come in if it wasn't safe. And we had to be safer sleeping in here than if we'd stayed outside.

Warmer, too.

Zane and Blake had created a circle in the center of the main area and lined the perimeter with rocks. We arranged the firewood in the middle of it, and I avoided meeting Zane's eyes, still feeling the heat on my back from how close I'd been to him when we'd fought together. It had felt even more intimate than sleeping in the same bed together—it was like our bodies had been one.

Once we finished arranging the firewood, Blake used his magic to light it up. His eyes glowed orange, and he stared intensely into the dancing flames, as if he was watching a moving picture inside of them. His forehead was furrowed, making him appear deep in thought.

Nicole sat down next to him and rested her head on his shoulder. "All okay?" she asked.

"Yeah," he said, still focused on the flames. "We should eat. Then we'll sleep in shifts, with one person awake at all times. That way, if anything tries to make its way in here, we'll be ready."

We divvied up the shifts, and then we ate, listening as Mason strategized a game plan for tomorrow. He was confident and mesmerizing while he spoke—even Blake and Nicole seemed to have full faith in his plans.

Mason was actually *so* confident that I was surprised they weren't wondering if he'd been to these mountains before. I watched them for any signs of suspicion, but there were none.

He truly had them snowed.

We chatted about the fight with the skeleton monsters as we ate, then laid out the thin blankets that had been stuffed in our bags and created makeshift pillows with some extra clothing. Instinctively, I laid my stuff next to Zane's. He gave me a small, approving smile, and warmth bloomed in my chest.

In moments like these, it was easy to forget the truth of what he was. But as it hit me again, I turned and held my hands up to warm them in the fire, even though Blake's magic had already warmed the cave to a comfortable temperature. But not *too* warm. Because as Mason had reminded us during dinner, we needed to stay bundled up in case something happened and we had to leave quickly.

Nicole and Blake laid their blankets next to each other, and Mason took the space closest to the cave's entrance.

Zane stepped up to join me next to the fire. "You fought well out there." He looked at the flames and not at me as he spoke.

"Thanks," I said, sneaking a glance as his strong, chiseled profile. "So did you."

He looked back at me, and I could tell he'd caught me checking him out.

"All right," Blake said, interrupting the moment. "We need our rest for tomorrow. As we know, I'm on first shift. You all should get some sleep."

As if to accentuate his point, he made the fire burn lower and dimmer, and we laid on our blankets to try to sleep.

The material was so thin that it was basically the same thing as sleeping on the ground. But the day must have exhausted me more than I'd realized, because with the warmth of the fire glowing on my face, and with a good amount of food in my stomach, sleep overtook me in seconds.

CHAPTER THIRTY-THREE

The rumbling started deep in my chest, expanding until the world was shaking.

My eyes snapped open.

The shaking intensified, like it was trying to jumble up my insides. It roared like a jet engine overhead, getting louder and louder. The walls cracked as they shifted, small stones crumbling to the ground.

What was happening?

My heart pounded, and my chest tightened, panic overtaking me as the walls started closing in.

From there, everything happened insanely quickly.

I tried to scramble up, but the shaking intensified and knocked me back to the ground.

Even though Zane was barely able to keep his footing, he grabbed my hand and pulled me up. The others screamed, but the rumbling muffled their voices. The moment I tried to see where their voices were coming from, my footing faltered, and I fell back to my knees.

This time, I picked myself back up, although Zane kept his hand in mine. He didn't leave my side, even though he could have gotten out of there far faster if he wasn't helping me.

Mason was ahead of us, also stumbling and falling as he tried to leave.

Blake and Nicole trailed behind.

The ceiling gave a loud *crack* as a split formed in the rocks above.

It was going to cave in.

We were going to die. And we didn't have enough time to get out.

I yanked my hand out of Zane's and held both of my hands over my head, as if I were strong enough to stop the rocks from crashing down on me.

No, I thought, and I held my breath, calling every last bit of power within me to gather the strength to protect us from being crushed.

It surged through my feet, all the way up to my hands until a beam of comforting, solid warmth flowed out of my open palms.

The shaking stopped.

The rocks that had come loose from the ceiling flung

outward, landing beyond us. A few pebbles clattered to the ground, and dirt puffed up like smoke. Other than that, everything seemed okay.

We breathed heavily, and the snapping of the fire echoed through the cave.

Somehow, throughout all of that, the campfire had kept burning. Nicole and Blake were huddled together beside it, holding each other close. From the looks of it, they hadn't even tried to run.

I glanced at the exit, relieved it hadn't caved in.

"How did you do that?" Zane studied me like he was trying to pry the secret out of my soul.

"I have no idea." I stared down at my hands, amazed and confused at the same time. "I just didn't want to get squished."

"You didn't do anything." Mason puffed his chest out proudly, his voice booming through the cave. "I used air magic to stop the rocks from hitting us."

I glanced up at the ceiling.

The crack was gone.

Impossible. Air magic could stop the rocks from hitting us, but it couldn't *repair a cave ceiling.*

I wasn't supposed to be able to repair a cave ceiling, either. But that magic had come from me. I knew it had.

But Mason was giving me a hard stare, as if telling me he knew I'd done it, but not to say anything.

Why did he want me to stay quiet?

I couldn't ask him here, in front of Nicole and Blake. I couldn't do anything he didn't want me to do in front of Nicole and Blake—unless I wanted to put their lives in danger. We were playing under Mason and Zane's rules. And if pretending I had nothing to do with whatever had just happened now was what it took to protect Nicole and Blake, then so be it.

From Zane's scowl, I had a feeling he was thinking the same thing.

"We need to get out of here," Nicole said, rolling up our makeshift beds and packing our bags. "That could have been a natural earthquake, but it also might not have been."

"You think the immortals caused an earthquake?" I hurried over to help her pack.

Blake was helping as well, but he was moving slowly, staring at the wall deep in thought. "We have no idea what they can do," he said. "But if they caused it, then they know we're here."

I flung my pack over my back and reached for my sword, gripping the handle in preparation to unsheathe it at any second. "You think they could be out there?" I looked at Zane as I asked the question, since he'd be the one to know.

As would Mason, but after whatever had just happened, I trusted him even less than I had before.

"It can't hurt to be ready," he said, his hand hovering over the handle of his own sword.

"If anything's out there, I doubt it's an immortal," Mason said confidently. "We took this path because Fulla said it's on the edge of the Immortal Mountains. They live nowhere near here. The worst it could be is a troll, and trolls are idiots. They have no fighting strategy whatsoever. Getting past them would be easy."

I thought back to the troll Alyssa and I had fought in the alley—it had been anything but *easy*.

Then again, I'd been basically untrained at that point. And while Alyssa had been through plenty of training, she'd frozen because she'd never truly had her life in danger in a fight.

But none of that mattered. Because if Mason said the immortals didn't come out here, then he was probably right. And the immortals had no reason to attack us, since they'd know we were traveling with two of their own.

"If it wasn't the immortals, then what was it?" I asked.

"We're in the mountains," Mason continued. "Mountains are known seismic zones. They get earthquakes out here. It could have been natural."

"It *could* have been," Nicole said in a way that made it obvious she didn't believe it. "In which case, we're safe. Relatively. But if something *did* cause it on purpose, then we're not getting anything done by staying in here like scared prey. We need to get out there and show them who they're messing with."

"That's my girl," Blake said proudly, and he looked around at the rest of us. "Are you all ready?"

"As ever." Mason smirked knowingly, and then he spun around and led the way out of the cave.

CHAPTER THIRTY-FOUR

The first rays of sunlight were peeking out over the trees when we stepped out of the cave. And as Mason had said, nothing was waiting for us out there. Nothing jumped out at us in an ambush, either.

But I didn't for a second think the earthquake had been natural. There was something bigger going on, and I was close to positive that Mason knew what it was. Unfortunately, I had no opportunities to ask him, since the group was staying together at all times. Strength in numbers and all of that.

We didn't move as fast today as we had yesterday. Blake had insisted on staying at the back of the pack to protect us, and he was going slower to remain as on-guard as possible.

It felt like we were hiking forever. The icy air made every second feel like an eternity, and my bones were so cold that I doubted I'd ever feel warm again. But somehow, I trooped on. I'd come this far—I wasn't going to collapse into a hypothermic heap now.

Eventually, the sky dimmed.

"There's a small clearing ahead," Mason said from the front of the pack. "We can set up camp there for the night. From the map Fulla showed me, we're far enough from the immortal village that they won't be able to see the smoke from our fire."

Like yesterday, I helped Mason and Nicole search for wood. I wanted some time with Mason to ask him about what had happened back in the cave—if he knew anything about why I'd been able to stop that earthquake and fix the crack in the ceiling—but Nicole stayed near me the entire time.

I could always ask him once we got back to the school.

We returned with firewood and placed it inside the rock circle that Blake and Zane had set up. They'd also already taken the goat meat out of the packs to get ready to eat. Dried meat was nowhere as good as the fresh meat we'd had yesterday, but we were in no position to be picky. Besides, my tongue was so cold that I couldn't taste much of anything, anyway.

We ate in near silence, exhausted from the day, and needing to preserve as much energy as possible.

"We should get some sleep," Nicole finally said. "If the

directions Fulla gave us are correct, we should reach the hammer by early evening if we leave at sunrise."

"The instructions are correct," Mason said, and then he glanced at Blake. His gaze was hard, as if he was waiting for something.

Blake took a deep breath and gazed into the fire. "The four of you need to leave at sunrise," he said. "I'll stay here and wait for you to return."

"What?" Nicole gasped. "Why?"

"I ran into a slight difficulty while we were fighting the draugr." He pulled at the bottom of his snow pants and lifted them up, revealing an inflamed, red wound on his calf, with black veiny lines coming out of the center of it. The wound had a half-moon shaped center, and it was decaying inward, like it was trying to eat its way to his bone.

"You were bitten," I said.

"Yes." He nodded. "It's been slowing me down, and it's getting worse. You won't make it to the hammer tomorrow if I'm holding you back."

"You should have told me." Nicole looked at him accusingly. "So I can try to heal it."

"It's an injury from a Norse monster." His eyes were sad. "Your magic won't work on it."

"That doesn't mean it's going to stop me from trying."

She rolled up her sleeves, rubbed her palms together, and rested them on the gruesome, painful-looking wound.

She held his gaze, deeply and intensely, then closed her eyes. Her face was as calm as ever as she concentrated on using her magic.

A full minute passed in silence.

During that time, I'd grabbed Zane's hand. Neither of us looked at each other, but our breathing was synced at the same, steady rate, as if our souls were as locked together as our fingers.

Eventually, Nicole opened her eyes and lifted her hands off Blake's leg.

The wound hadn't changed.

Tears welled in her eyes, and she buried her face in her hands.

Panic rushed through me. Because I'd never seen Nicole so vulnerable with her emotions. As the only other female in the group, was I supposed to do something to try to comfort her? Hug her or something?

Not like I thought an awkward hug would help anything.

I didn't have to contemplate it for long, because Blake reached for her, pulled her face to his, and gave her a long, slow kiss—as if they were the only ones in the clearing.

I looked away, not wanting to intrude on their private moment.

My eyes accidentally met Zane's, and my heart stopped as I zeroed in on his lips, wanting him to kiss me as passionately as Blake was kissing Nicole.

At the same time, I was grateful he wasn't the one who was injured. Which was a horrible thing to think, since I didn't wish either of them ill. So I tried to push it from my mind.

Especially because *Zane could heal Blake.*

The reminder was a punch to my gut.

"There has to be something we can do." I kept my voice slow and steady, focusing on Zane.

I wanted to send the thought into his mind: *heal him.*

"The poison looks like it's moving slowly," Zane said, as if he had experience with this sort of thing. "If we head out early tomorrow and meet you back here at night with the hammer, we should be able to get you back to the school quickly enough for them to do everything they can to help you. In the meantime…." He stood, walked to the edge of the campsite, and gathered some snow into a ball. "Keep this on your leg. The cold should slow down the poison."

Disappointment flowed through me.

Zane wasn't going to heal Blake.

I gave Zane a lethal stare. "Do you think that will be enough?" I asked, my soul feeling dead as I spoke the words.

Because he had to do more than this.

He was *better* than this. He had to be. He wouldn't leave Blake out in the cold to die.

Or would he?

I kept hoping his soul was different, but I also knew that whatever bond I shared with him made me biased. Zane was no better than what he'd told me of the immortals when we were in that boat together. He was proving it right now.

I could reveal his secret. Right now. I could tell Nicole and Blake everything.

And then what? Have them tie Zane down and slice his wrist so Blake could drink his blood? And once Blake was healed, what would they do from there? Kill Zane? Kill Mason?

No—they didn't know that Mason was also an immortal.

Mason would kill Nicole and Blake before they had a shot at Zane.

Maybe I was underestimating Nicole and Blake. After all, Nicole was a demigod. As was I. Surely we had a chance against Mason.

But I wouldn't be able to hurt Zane.

If they tried to kill him, what would I do? Whose side would I take?

I knew the right, moral answer.

But in this circumstance, I didn't trust my body and soul to go against Zane.

Which meant I was back to where I always seemed to end up—keeping Zane's secret. Even as Blake was lying here, possibly dying, I was siding with Zane.

I hated myself more than ever.

"The snow will slow the poison from spreading," Zane repeated, looking to Nicole for her opinion.

"It makes sense, in theory," she said. "And I'll see if it works, because I'm staying here with Blake. The three of you will continue in the morning without us."

"I'll be fine here by myself," Blake insisted. "You need to go with them. They need you to help them get the hammer."

"I'm not leaving you alone like this." Her eyes were sharper and deadlier than I'd ever seen them. "The three of them are strong. They can do this. But I'm here for you, always. And you're in no shape to force me to do anything." She chuckled a bit after that last part, even though it was anything but funny. "So, I'm staying here whether you want me to or not."

I expected him to insist again that she go with us, but he gave her a single nod of acceptance.

He must have known how bad it was.

"It's decided then," Mason said. "We'll leave at dawn. And then, by nightfall, we'll return with the hammer and figure out a way to get Blake back down this mountain."

CHAPTER THIRTY-FIVE

We woke at sunrise the next morning, and Blake lifted the bottom of his pants so we could check on his injury. He winced in pain, and I could smell the infection the moment the wound was exposed to the open air.

It had progressed so the black veins nearly reached his knee. The skin around the bite was decaying further, eating away at his skin.

Nicole grabbed another ball of snow and pressed it to the wound. "Keep this here," she said, and then she looked desperately at Zane. "You have ice magic. Is there anything you can do? Can you freeze it to stop it from expanding?"

"I can try," he said, his expression giving away nothing. "If the skin suffers severe frostbite, it could kill the infection. But you might never be able to use your leg again." He looked at Blake as he said the last part, leaving the decision up to him.

Blake clenched his jaw, and his gaze hardened. "Do it."

Nicole pressed her lips together, saying nothing. She just reached for Blake's hand and held it in support.

Zane walked over to Blake, his palms hovering above the wound. "Are you sure? Once it's done, I won't be able to reverse it."

A lie.

I curled my hands into fists tight enough that I nearly lost all sensation in my fingers.

"Do it and get it over with," Blake said.

Zane placed his palms on the wound, and a slight, ice-blue light glowed from underneath them.

Blake ground his teeth together, a low rumble of pain sounding from his chest.

Mason just stood to the side. He watched the scene with what looked like amusement, as if he were an immortal psychopath.

At least Zane looked somewhat guilty.

When he lifted his hands, the skin around Blake's wound was so frostbitten that it was totally black.

Dead.

Tears welled in Nicole's eyes again, and she pulled Blake closer. "Once we're back, we'll figure out how to fix it," she said. "But at least for now, you're okay. You have to be okay."

"We'll figure it out," Blake assured her.

She nodded, although she didn't look totally convinced.

"The sun is almost fully risen," Mason broke into the conversation. "We should get a move on." He gathered his pack, antsy to head out.

I didn't look at either Zane or Mason when I picked mine up. Because by going into the Immortal Mountains with two immortals, I was either being very trusting or very stupid.

But you know what would be more stupid? Choosing to stay with Nicole and Blake, and leaving Mason and Zane to complete the mission on their own. Who knew what they'd do?

At least Blake had his fire magic to keep them warm. And Nicole was an excellent huntress, so the possibilities of them starving or freezing to death were two fewer things to worry about.

But worrying would get me nowhere. The best thing I could do for them was to help get the hammer so we could return to the academy as quickly as possible, where Blake could receive the medical attention he needed.

Except he has what he needs right here.

My eyes darted to Zane.

On our way up the mountain, I needed to convince him to heal Blake. His decision would prove if he was truly a monster, or if he actually had a soul.

I took a deep breath and looked at Nicole and Blake. She was curled up next to him, her arms wrapped around him as if she was afraid she could lose him at any minute. He was stiffly sitting up, barely receptive to her affection.

"Every minute we spend here is one wasted when we could be getting closer to the hammer," I said, sounding far fiercer than I'd imagined I would. "Let's get going. We'll be back tonight with the hammer, and we can figure the rest out from there."

I glanced at Zane when I said that final part, and his eyes met mine for a split second before he looked away. But in that split second, his eyes had flashed with guilt.

Monsters didn't feel guilt.

He had it in his heart to change his mind. I knew he did.

And as crazy as it was, I believed in him, even though he'd given me every reason to feel otherwise.

"Good luck." Nicole managed the tiniest of smiles, but her gray eyes looked empty and dead.

It wasn't a look I liked to see on her. But then I saw a flash of something else. Hope.

Nicole was strong, but sometimes strength wasn't going out to fight and kill your enemy.

Sometimes, strength was staying back to be with the ones you loved when they needed you the most, and trusting others to pick up the slack without you.

"Thanks," I said, strong and steady. "You can count on us. I promise."

"I know I can."

We shared an understanding look, and then, Zane, Mason, and I set off to continue our journey up the mountain.

CHAPTER THIRTY-SIX

As he had since we'd started our journey up the mountains, Mason led the way.

Zane insisted on keeping us safe from behind, which left me in the middle.

Even though Nicole and Blake didn't have superhuman hearing (at least, I didn't think they did), I waited until we were a few miles away from camp before stopping and turning to face Zane.

I hoped my eyes were as icy as the snow around us.

"You could have healed him," I said simply.

He stopped immediately, although he felt far away, like there was a glass wall between us.

A wall that would forever keep us from being on the same side, no matter how much we tried to pretend it wasn't there.

"I kept him alive." His words sounded sharp and rehearsed.

"For now," I said. "You don't know how long it will hold."

"It will hold for long enough."

"What does that even *mean?*" I was no longer calm, and I didn't care. "Long enough that he'll be able to get medical care that might heal him—if that even exists? Or long enough so you can help him get back to the academy—which would fulfill the promise you made to me—so he can die there?" The rage inside me grew hotter the more I spoke.

"We'll be able to get back to the academy," he said. "Where he can get medical care."

"But not the type of care that will heal him so he'll be able to walk again. Because I'm not a medical professional, but it doesn't look like he'll be able to keep that leg." I narrowed my eyes and held the silence between us, daring him to refute my statement.

He said nothing.

"It's more than just the leg," I realized, even though it wasn't what I wanted to be true. "You only slowed down the progression of the poison. He's going to die. It's just going to be slower than it would have been otherwise."

"Correct." Mason's voice boomed from behind me, and when I spun around to look at him, he was smiling.

"Seriously?" I asked. "You're enjoying this?"

"Are you surprised?" His smile twisted into one of complete cruelty.

"I hate you," I said, and then I returned my attention back to Zane. "And I'll hate you forever if you don't use your magic to heal him."

He flinched—the only show of emotion he'd given all morning—and breathed slowly and steadily as he held my gaze. "You do realize what you're asking of me," he finally said. "Right?"

"I'm asking you to trust Nicole and Blake." I made it sound simple, even though we all knew it was far more complicated than that.

Zane's eyes remained hard.

Mason slithered around to stand next to him. "Your naivety is showing, young demigod," he hissed, looking at me like a fly he was about to trap. "Your magic might be strong, but if you want to survive the upcoming war, you need to be far more strategic than this."

I reached for the handle of the Golden Sword, and it took all my restraint to not unsheathe it and test how easily it could slice through an immortal's neck. Magic rushed through me, urging me to stop holding back.

"You don't truly think you could fight me." Mason shook his head and clucked his tongue in disappointment.

Zane was by my side in a second, and he placed his hand on top of the one I was using to hold the sword.

"Careful," he said, his breath cool and minty as it fluttered across my cheek.

I forced myself to remain focused on Mason and not look over at Zane—and not lean into Zane, despite every nerve in my body wanting to do so.

I didn't need Zane's protection. I *wanted* it—because I wanted to be able to trust him—but I didn't *need* it. They were entirely different things.

"I'm not going to fight you, but I do believe I could," I said once my thoughts felt somewhat more organized.

"Anyone *can* fight anyone." Mason smirked. "It doesn't mean they'll win."

"True," I said. "But we both know I'm stronger than you thought. You might think you're the smartest person in every room, but you were just as surprised in the cave as I was."

Zane released his hold on my hand and stepped away. "What are you talking about?" He looked to me, then Mason, then back again.

"An excellent question," Mason said. "Why don't you tell your *soulmate* what you're referring to?"

I hated the way he said *soulmate*—like he was making a mockery of it. Like he thought the universe was playing a giant joke on everyone by making me and Zane soulmates.

And as much as I hated to agree with any of Mason's thoughts, I couldn't argue with that one.

Zane watched me patiently, as if we had all the time in the world. And to him, maybe we did. He was an immortal, after all. The passing of time must feel like nothing to him.

"I'm the one who saved us from being crushed in the cave," I said, overly aware of how ridiculous it sounded the moment I spoke the words. "It wasn't Mason. It was me."

"Why do you think that?" If Zane thought it was ridiculous, there wasn't so much as a hint of it in his tone.

"Because I felt the magic. I connected with the ground, and with the walls of the cave, and with the rocks. It's hard to explain exactly what happened, but I pushed out the magic, prayed that we wouldn't get crushed, and then..." I left the sentence hanging, since we all knew what had happened in the cave. I looked to Mason, and continued, "You know I did it. You gave me a look like you were asking me to not tell Nicole and Blake."

"Because you used earth magic," he said simply.

"How?" I stared at him, baffled.

"That's a good question," he said. "I don't know the answer. But it would lead to discussions that would distract us from our mission, and getting the hammer is our priority."

I looked to Zane to see what he thought. He was watching me with curiosity, like I was a puzzle he couldn't figure out.

"It could have something do with Hades and his affinity for precious stones," Zane theorized. "But those caves are rocks—not gems."

"Like I said—it was earth magic," Mason said. "And now we're standing here talking about your magic instead of focusing on finding the hammer. But we're not going to get any answers about it right now. Which is why we need to table this discussion for when we get back to the academy."

I shivered in the cold, and while I hated to admit it, Mason's point was valid. The sooner we got the hammer, the sooner we could get out of here and move forward.

"Fine." I focused on Zane again. "But think about what I said. It's not too late to save Blake."

"I know." His answer was so neutral that it felt empty.

Unable to look at him anymore, I spun around and started walking again. Mason eagerly continued to lead us, picking up the pace, and we didn't talk at all for the next few hours.

As we walked, my mind spun.

Why did I have earth magic? Maybe it had to do with my mom being Hecate? My mom had always been connected to the world around her. But we weren't genetically related. She'd confirmed it when we'd spoken in the cottage.

Unless she'd been lying?

Maybe. It seemed like my entire life was a lie nowadays.

Eventually, we took a break for food and water. I didn't bring up my earth magic again, and neither did they. We ate in a tense silence.

It didn't seem like they had any answers, but I had no reason to trust anything they said. I wanted to believe Zane, but whatever trust I'd started forming with him had broken when he'd refused to heal Blake. With it, my heart felt broken as well.

Hopefully we'd get to the hammer soon. I didn't want to be out here with the two of them any longer than necessary.

Then, as I was thinking about the hammer, something tugged at the back of my mind. Metal. Like it had latched onto my brain like a fishing line and was trying to pull me closer.

I dropped my plate onto my lap and stared straight ahead. "It's close," I said.

"What's close?" Zane asked.

"Thor's Hammer."

He watched me quizzically. "How do you know?"

I met his gaze, steady and sure. "Because I can feel it."

CHAPTER THIRTY-SEVEN

I didn't lead them along the natural path—instead, I made my own way through the trees, following the direct line to the hammer. I didn't need a map. All I needed was my magic and intuition. It was like I was hypnotized, and getting the hammer was the only thing I could focus on. I was so locked in to reaching it that I was barely even processing how cold I was.

I was breathing heavily once I reached the clearing in the woods where the buzzing of metal was so strong that it traveled into the soles of my feet and reverberated through my body.

I stepped into the clearing, and three creatures emerged from the thick trees surrounding it.

Wolves. *Giant* wolves about three times the size of regular ones. Their eyes glowed yellow, and they bared their sharp teeth, growling at us like they wanted to rip us to shreds and eat us for dinner. They prowled forward and stood in the center of the clearing—right above where the hammer was buried. They stopped there, but the expression in their ferocious eyes was clear.

Try to get closer, and they'd attack.

I reached for the hilt of the Golden Sword and felt for the hammer with my mind.

Zane stepped in front of me before I could unsheathe the sword. It was like he knew where my mind was going, and he wanted me to stop.

"She's one of us," he said to them calmly, not turning around to look at me as he spoke. "Harm her, and you're dead."

The wolves whined in submission, backed up, and sat down.

"You can let go of your sword," he told me, although he remained tense, still not looking back at me. "These wolves are products of the immortals. We're their masters, and they submit to us."

"What do you mean that they're 'products?'" I asked.

"They're the result of breeding immortals and trolls. We've found that they're excellent guard dogs."

"Oh. That's... good," I said, even though it sounded like a crossbreeding experiment gone wrong.

The "good" part I was referring to was that they wouldn't attack. Because despite everything else I'd fought and killed recently, I still didn't want to go up against them.

I'd never been a person who sought out violence and confrontation, and despite finding out that Hades was my father, I had no interest in letting that change. Although from what I'd learned about Hades, he was a hermit down there in the Underworld. So maybe it made sense.

Mason walked to the center of the clearing and knelt in the snow. It melted away around him, revealing the muddy earth below.

No longer frozen in the solid dirt, the hammer's magic flowed out of the ground, calling to me, begging to be set free. I held up a hand and pulled at the invisible fishing line in my mind, loosening the hammer from the earth and drawing it out towards me.

It exploded out of the ground and flew at me, the metal handle smacking into my palm like magnets snapping together.

Unthinkable power rushed through me as visible electricity buzzed around the hammer's giant metal head. The Golden Sword pulsed by my side. I had two weapons made for gods, and I felt unstoppable as the wind whipped around me like I was in the center of a small tornado.

A tornado of magic. I held the hammer with both hands, and its power flooded my veins, filling me up more than I'd ever thought possible. I was ball of lightning ready to explode, and it was absolutely incredible.

Someone said my name in a muffled voice nearby, but I ignored it, staring at the glowing weapon in my hand and reveling in the fact that we'd completed what we'd come here to do.

Thor's Hammer was *mine*.

Suddenly, someone flashed in front of me and reached for my shoulders, shaking me.

Mason.

"Summer!" he screamed to be heard above the wind, staring at me with greed in his eyes. "We had a deal."

I tried to free myself from his hold, but he was far stronger than me. I could barely budge.

"Give me the hammer," he growled. "Or I'll go back to where Nicole is nursing Blake's wound and kill both of them before you can blink."

The threat pulled me out of the magical high from the hammer, and the wind slowed around me. My grip remained tight on the hammer's handle, but Mason's words echoed in my mind.

He'd kill Nicole and Blake.

With both the hammer and the sword, it was possible that I could stop him. And if I could kill him—which was a big if, since I didn't know anything about how to kill an immortal—what then?

I supposed we could blame Mason's death on the wolves. Say we'd fought them, and he'd been a casualty.

But the "we" I was thinking about was me and Zane. I was assuming he'd be on my side, even though given that he and Mason were both immortals, he was technically on Mason's side.

"You can't fight me." Mason's eyes bled into mine, his pupils so dilated that his irises appeared almost black. It was like they were leaking into my soul and poisoning me with their malice. "You're a demigod. I'm an immortal. Hand the hammer over to me, and I'll get you and your friends back to the academy safely."

I was trapped in his hold, his grip so strong on my shoulders that he could crush my bones in a heartbeat. "How can I trust you?" I asked, the words getting stuck in my throat.

He leered at me. "Do you trust that I'm going to kill your friends if you don't do as you promised?"

"Yes," I answered automatically.

"Then that should be enough for you to keep your word and honor our deal."

I blinked a few times, trying to get myself together. "Why do you want the hammer so badly?" I asked.

"Easy." He smirked again. "You're already holding the Golden Sword of Athena. If you take charge of the hammer as well, it makes you too much of a threat. And I know your feelings for me are… less than loving, shall we say? We need to even the playing field."

"So you *do* think I could fight you." I couldn't help but smirk in return.

"Oh, I'd win. But it wouldn't do us any good to find out."

I stilled, struggling with the idea of parting with the hammer. Electricity continued to buzz around it, and I had a feeling it didn't want me to hand it over to Mason. It liked me. Probably because of my affinity for metal.

"Summer," Zane said, his voice calm and razor sharp. "You made a deal. Immortals don't like it when people go back on their deals."

"You should listen to your soulmate." Again, the way Mason said it grated on me. "I'm growing impatient. Do you want your friends down there to survive? Or should I zip out of here and kill them right now?" His eyes gleamed, like he was enjoying the thought of murdering Nicole and Blake.

If that happened, their deaths would be my fault. All because I didn't want Mason to be the one to transport the hammer back to the academy. And Zane had a point—I'd made a promise to Mason. Did I really want to get on the bad side of an immortal?

"Here." I thrust it forward for him to take before I could second guess myself.

His eyes gleamed like a child's on Christmas morning

as he reached for the hammer and pried it from my hands. My body urged me to resist, but I fought it and let him take it.

He gazed at it in wonder, smiling like he was holding the key to the world. Then he took a few steps back and glanced at the three giant wolves sitting patiently, watching this entire scene go down.

"Fenrir," he said. "Come."

A gray wolf twice the size of the other massive ones slinked out of the forest. It was like he'd come out of nowhere. Yes, the trees were thick, but how did I not see him before?

Zane cursed, sucked in a sharp breath, and reached for my hand, squeezing it tight.

The air shimmered and blurred around Mason, and suddenly, I wasn't looking at Mason anymore. Because he was shorter and paler now, with long, slick black hair and inky eyes to match.

He smirked again, and in his new form, he looked more devious than ever. "My brother's going to get such a kick out of this," he said, and then he jumped onto the giant wolf's back, and they ran off into the forest and disappeared.

CHAPTER THIRTY-EIGHT

The other wolves followed Mason and the giant wolf—Fenrir—into the forest.

I blinked and stared at my hands that had been holding the hammer a minute earlier.

"What just happened?" I asked Zane, shocked at how quickly it had all gone down.

"That wasn't Mason," he said simply.

"I gathered that." The image of his creepy, pinpoint black eyes refused to leave my mind. "But you recognized him. The *real* him. Assuming the person he transformed into was really him?"

This was getting more confusing by the second.

"That was him, all right." He ran his fingers through his hair and started pacing back and forth. "I knew something was off about Mason, but I assumed it was because he was one of my uncle's guards sent to keep watch over me. I didn't think it was *that*."

"That it was *what*?" I asked, needing him to keep talking.

"That person wasn't Mason. It was Loki," he said. "Thor's brother."

I took a moment to let that sink in. Because I was no expert in Norse mythology, but I'd heard enough about Loki in pop culture to know he was a major player.

"You didn't know about this before now?" I asked, hoping with everything inside me that this wasn't another secret he'd been keeping.

"I didn't," he said. "I swear it."

As much as I knew I should doubt everything he said, I could tell by his initial reaction to Loki's reveal that he was telling the truth. Relief passed through me at the confirmation that he hadn't been lying about yet *another* thing.

"Okay," I said, and he nodded, looking thankful that I took him for his word. "How did he do... that?" I motioned to the general area in front of me where Mason had changed his appearance.

"Loki can shapeshift," Zane said simply. "He enjoys using this talent to trick others. Because that's one of his favorite things to do—trick and deceive. He's the god of trickery." He sneered, his obvious hate for Loki leaking through his tone.

"So he's been pretending to be Mason all this time."

"I don't know when he started posing as Mason," he said. "But yes, he's been pretending."

"What happened to the real Mason?"

"I have no idea." Zane said. "He's probably dead."

He said it so casually, as if it didn't bother him that Loki had killed someone and slipped into his place.

"You think he'd been pretending to be Mason for a while?" I asked.

"Possibly," Zane said. "I never knew Mason well, and like I said, Loki's the master of deception. It's impossible to know."

"He didn't change much in the time that I've known him," I said. "So I'm guessing I never knew the real Mason at all."

"Probably not."

I glanced back into the forest. "Do you think we can catch up to him before he gets away with the hammer?"

After saying it, I realized how crazy it was. Especially since he'd already gotten far enough that I could no longer feel the hammer with my mind. "Never mind," I said before Zane could answer. "Going up against a god probably isn't a good idea."

"Agreed," Zane said. "Although technically, Loki's half god, and half immortal. But he's considered a god despite that."

"Oh," I said. "So he *is* one of you. Sort of."

"Absolutely not." Zane sneered. "We don't count Loki as one of our own. He's not fully accepted by the gods, either. How he's remained alive after all the stunts he's pulled is beyond me. But he gets away with everything. Thus, the trickster god."

"And the wolves listen to him more than the immortals," I said, assuming it had to be true after what I'd just seen.

"That wasn't just any wolf," he said. "Fenrir is Loki's son."

I flinched back and balked. "How...?" I asked, since that was too insane to possibly be true. Then I remembered that wolves were the result of immortals bred with trolls. "He hooked up with a troll?"

"With an immortal," he said simply.

Nausea crept up on me as I looked at the place where Fenrir had been standing. *"That's* what happens when immortals have children with gods?" I asked, my heart lurching into my throat.

Not that I was thinking about what possible children with Zane would be like.

Nope. Definitely not. I hated him. He looked like a beautiful, mesmerizing immortal on the outside, but he was a monster on the inside. I couldn't let myself forget that.

"That's what happens when an immortal has a child with *Loki,*" he said. "Don't worry. All other children of gods and immortals turn out perfectly normal. Powerful and magical, but they're human in appearance."

"Okay." I nodded, not wanting to look like it mattered to me. Because Zane and I would *not* be participating in any activities that would result in children.

My cheeks heated. Was I really thinking about sex with Zane at a time like this?

There was something seriously wrong with my brain.

Stupid soulmate bond.

And judging by the intense way he was gazing down at me, I had a feeling his mind was in the exact same place.

"Anyway." I stepped back, sucked in a long breath of the freezing air, and straightened, desperate to change the subject. "What happens now that Mason—*Loki*—has the hammer?"

It was going to take time to adjust to the fact that Mason wasn't really Mason.

"Loki's unpredictable," he said. "He's probably trying to goad his brother, but there's no way to know his true motives. For all we know, he's the one who found the hammer and buried it, and then he took us up here for entertainment."

"You really think he'd do that?" I asked.

"He's the trickster god. Like I said—he's unpredictable."

I pursed my lips at the thought of how twisted that

would be. It meant he'd known exactly what we were walking into, and what had happened to Blake was all for his *entertainment*.

"We need to get back and check on the others," I said. "They need to know what happened up here. And we have to get them back to the school."

I sharpened my gaze and turned around, not looking back at Zane as I started to make my way back down the mountain.

CHAPTER THIRTY-NINE

Zane filled me in on Loki as we walked. It seemed like every conflict in Norse mythology was caused by Loki, or at least involved Loki. The craziest part was that Loki got away with it every time, with basically no repercussions.

How could these people allow themselves to continue getting tricked like that?

Finally, we made it back to the clearing.

Blake was laying on a blanket, looking paler than ever. The fire in the center of camp was dimmer than it had been when we'd left. Nicole sat between Blake and the fire, her legs pulled to her chest and her arms wrapped around them, shivering. Blake's pants covered his wound, but judging by how corpse-like he looked, I assumed it had gotten worse.

Nicole lifted her head to look at us when we walked back into the clearing.

The hope in her eyes disappeared instantly.

"Where's Mason?" she asked. "And the hammer?"

I sat down with them and summed up everything that had happened as quickly as possible.

When I finished, Nicole's expression was pure shock.

"Wow," she said. "Just... wow."

"Exactly." I looked to Blake, who'd been drifting in and out of consciousness. "How's he doing?" I asked Nicole, since Blake didn't seem with it enough to answer for himself. Plus, the answer was obvious. It just seemed impolite to not ask.

"Not good." She sighed in defeat. "He can't go anywhere like this. I don't know how we can get him back to the academy."

"I'll be okay in the morning," Blake mumbled. "I just need to rest. It'll be okay."

Nicole sniffed and wiped tears off her cheeks. "The two of you need to go back without us and get help."

"No," I said immediately. "You'll die up here."

"Maybe. Maybe not." She shrugged. "But the four of us staying here does nothing. If you go back, at least we'll have a chance."

"That's not true." I zeroed in on Zane, who actually had the audacity to look guilty.

He was sitting here next to Blake, watching him die,

perfectly able to save him, and looking *guilty* about not doing anything.

"Are you really going to leave him here to die?" My frustration boiled over, and the words left my mouth before I could stop them.

Because Zane was better than this.

He had to be.

The universe wouldn't make me soulmates with someone this cruel.

"You have to save him," I begged, surprised when his eyes softened. "Please."

Nicole looked back and forth between us in confusion. "What are you talking about?" she asked.

I kept my gaze locked on Zane's. Because this was too much.

If he wouldn't tell them, then I would. Either way, Nicole and Blake were likely dead. The only difference would be if Zane killed them in cold blood to make sure his secret wouldn't get out, or if he walked away and left them to die alone. I'd go with him back to the school to get help—I wouldn't be able to do any good staying here—but their chance of survival would be slim to none.

At least this way, I'd have done everything I could.

I opened my mouth to tell Nicole the truth, but before I could, Zane took his dagger to his wrist and slit it, his blood escaping through the opening.

Nicole's brow scrunched in confusion. "What are you

doing?" she asked, growing quiet when Zane lowered his wrist to Blake's pale lips and let the blood flow into his mouth.

"Saving Blake's life." Zane refused to look at either of us when he spoke.

I watched in amazement as color crept back into Blake's face. A few seconds passed, and Zane pulled his wrist away, leaving blood smeared on Blake's lips.

Nicole leaned over Blake and cupped his cheeks with her hands, gazing at him with wonder, amazement, and love. It was as if she were breathing life into him herself. She brushed his reddened lips with her fingers, wiping the blood from them.

Blake's shallow breaths grew steadier. He groaned, like he was waking up from a deep sleep, and used his hands to sit up, looking around in a daze.

"What happened?" he asked Nicole, who was holding one of his hands as if she thought he'd fall dead if she let go. "Did you just heal me with your blood?"

"It wasn't my blood." She paused, as if she was coming to terms with what had just happened. "It was Zane's."

Blake brushed his fingers over his lips. Then he looked at Zane, his fiery eyes hard. "Start talking."

"I don't just have ice magic," Zane said, surely and steadily, as if he'd practiced this a million times. "I can also heal."

Blake stood, taking Nicole with him, so they towered over us.

We jumped up as well, and it was like there was a crackling, invisible wall between us, painting us as their enemies.

"Your blood heals Norse injuries." Blake's eyes blazed with anger as he stared down Zane, ready to fight. "You knew what those skeleton zombies were and how to kill them. You know your way through these mountains. You're far stronger than any other student at the school—your performance during Greek Week made that clear. You're not one of us. You're one of them."

The accusation hung heavily in the air.

Zane was so still that he didn't appear to be breathing.

Nicole's eyes darted to her bow and arrows, which were laid out by the fire.

"I'm not going to hurt you," Zane said, an edge of warning in his tone. "If I wanted to hurt you, then I wouldn't have healed you. I'm not your enemy."

"You're a Norse god," Blake said. "That makes you our enemy."

"I'm not a god," Zane said simply.

"Then what are you?"

"I'm an immortal. More commonly known as a Giant in mythology."

"In *Norse* mythology." Blake sneered.

"Yes." Zane nodded, somehow remaining calm. "But

my people dislike the gods as much as you do. We're on the same side."

"We are *not* on the same side." Blake stepped forward, fireballs burning in his hands.

"Blake." Nicole placed her hand on his arm to get him to calm down. "He just saved your life. Let him talk."

Blake was so angry that it looked like his veins were going to pop out of his neck. But he took a few deep breaths, and the fireballs disappeared.

I released the breath I'd been holding, and my arm brushed Zane's.

I hadn't realized I'd edged so close to him.

I stepped to the side, hoping they hadn't noticed.

But Nicole was quicker than that. "You knew about this," she said simply.

At once, all eyes were on me. Blake and Nicole, betrayed. And Zane, more comforting than ever, as if telling me he'd understand if I told them everything.

It spilled out of me like a dam that had been broken, starting with Zane helping me kill Lin when she attacked us at the academy, and ending with Mason assisting us in cleaning up Fulla and Vera's murders.

But it was an edited version of the truth. Because I left out everything Zane had told me at the lake—about how the immortals wanted to rule over both the Greek and Norse gods.

I made it sound like he was on our side.

I was protecting him.

Or I was protecting Blake and Nicole. Because if they knew everything, surely they'd try to kill him, regardless of his saving Blake's life. And Zane was far deadlier than they realized. If they tried to kill him, I'd bet on Zane winning that fight.

Along with that, I didn't want to turn Zane in. Not after he'd shown humanity by saving Blake's life—and Alyssa's as well. If I could get through to him about saving them, maybe I could get through to him about everything else. Maybe he wasn't the monster I'd thought he was.

"He turned on Lin and Vera for me," I finished, praying that what I'd told Nicole and Blake would be enough for them to understand. "He's with us now."

Disgust rippled through me. Because Zane had done what he'd done for *me*—not because he cared about the Greeks.

"Very interesting." Blake kept his eyes leveled with Zane's. He didn't appear convinced, but he also wasn't holding fireballs in preparation to fight, which I supposed was a start. "But if you dislike the Norse gods as much as you claim, why not come forward and team up? Why hide in the shadows and spy on us?"

"Remember—as of a few weeks ago, you didn't know that the Norse gods had risen," Zane said. "We needed to gather information before coming forward and proposing our alliance."

"And when was that going to be?" Nicole asked.

"Whenever I was told to do so by my superiors."

Silence descended upon us for the first time since I'd told them about Zane.

"I understand that after all of this, it's difficult to trust me," he said carefully.

Blake scoffed. "The only thing stopping me from killing you right now is the fact that you just saved my life."

"I'm grateful for that." Zane smiled knowingly—the kind of smile that showed he knew that if he went up against Blake and Nicole, he'd win that fight. "And to further earn your trust, I'm going to give you information that will help you in the upcoming war."

CHAPTER FORTY

"I'm listening," Blake said.

"Not all the Norse gods have risen yet," he said. "Odin and his Valkyries are still buried beneath the earth. The gods are laying low as they try to get them out, but once they do, there'll be nothing stopping them from launching their attack."

"Odin—the King of the Gods in Norse mythology," Nicole said, since we'd all been brushing up on our Norse mythology recently. "Your equivalent of Zeus."

"There are many differences between Odin and Zeus," Zane said. "But yes—they're both the kings of their gods. And the Valkyries are Odin's warriors. Once they're freed, they *will* make themselves known."

"Why are you telling us this?" Blake asked, an edge of suspicion in his tone.

"To earn your trust," Zane repeated. "To give you an advantage when Odin and his Valkyries rise."

"*If* they rise," Nicole said. "We can try to stop it from happening."

"You can," Zane agreed.

"And how do we know you're telling the truth?" Blake asked.

"Trust," Zane said, and it took all my effort not to scoff.

If Blake and Nicole knew what was best for them, they'd see Zane for what he truly was.

From the suspicious look in Blake's eyes, I could tell he was doing just that.

"You saved Blake and Alyssa's lives." Nicole stepped forward, as if making a truce. "You turned on one of your own to save Summer's life." She glanced at me, and I nodded, confirming that it was true. "And now you're telling us important information to give us an advantage against the Norse gods. I think it's only logical that we give you the benefit of the doubt. And I'm sure Kate will agree."

"You're telling Kate?" I asked, caught off-guard.

"Of course." Nicole sounded surprised that I'd questioned it. "Kate is reasonable. There's nothing to worry about. She'll understand."

I glanced at Zane, who didn't appear worried in the slightest.

"We'll go to her immediately once we get back," he said. "After all the research she's been doing, I'm sure she'll have some ideas about where we can find the resting spot of Odin and the Valkyries."

"I'm glad we're on the same page," Nicole said. "Now, how about we head back down? After everything we just went through, it would be a shame if we ended up freezing to death because we didn't get a move on quickly enough."

Blake lit a fireball in his hand. "I can't freeze to death," he said. "I've got heat in my veins."

"And I've got ice," Zane said. "You can't freeze something that's already frozen."

Was it just me, or were they sort of... getting along?

"Well, I'm not as lucky as the two of you." I wrapped my arms around myself and shivered for emphasis. "Let's head back. The sooner we get to the academy, the sooner we can figure out our next steps."

"I like the way you think," Nicole said, and together, the four of us gathered our stuff and made our way down the mountain. We needed to stop for one more overnight, and by sunset the next day, we were back at the car.

Nicole, Blake, and I immediately started stripping off our outer layers. Zane didn't seem to notice the change in temperature—probably because he was naturally cold already.

We packed our stuff into the trunk, and Blake got into the driver's side, and Nicole into the passenger's side.

Zane rushed to the back door and opened it, motioning for me to go inside.

"Thanks," I said, sliding awkwardly into the back seat.

"Anytime," he said calmly, and he kept his eyes locked on mine, gazing down at me with so much intensity that it was like he was seeing every single part of me, down to the depths of my soul. "I love you, Summer Donovan."

He said it like it was a fact. Like it was something obvious I should already know.

I sat there, stunned, and sucked in a sharp breath, replaying the words in my mind. Because it was one thing to know we were soulmates. Being soulmates wasn't something we could choose.

But love? That was entirely different.

Did I love Zane?

I didn't know. My feelings for him were a confusing mess I'd been unable to sort through in my mind.

How could I love someone if I didn't trust them?

But while I didn't trust Zane to always tell the truth, I *did* trust him with my life. That had to count for something.

"It's okay—you don't have to say it back," he said quickly. "I just wanted you to know. And there's one more thing..." He paused, and I realized that Blake and Nicole were sitting quietly in their seats, pretending—and failing

—to look like they weren't hearing this conversation. "Thor's Hammer created electricity for you when you held it."

"Yeah," I stumbled over the word, feeling all over the place after Zane's confession.

He kept his gaze locked on mine, as serious as ever. "The hammer only creates electricity when it's held by a god."

I opened my mouth to tell him that didn't make any sense—that it must react that way for demigods, too.

But I only got two words in before he spun on his heel and ran back through the arch and into the forest, so quickly that he was a blur.

I stared at the place where he'd been in shock.

Where was he going? Did he leave something back in the forest? And if so, wouldn't he have said something instead of just disappearing like that?

Then it hit me—he was leaving me. He was running away from me.

No.

I jumped out of the car and ran through the arch, screaming his name and crying out for him to wait for me. The freezing air hit me like a sledgehammer. I kept running, searching for footsteps left in the snow, or flashes of him in the trees, but there was nothing. It was like he'd flashed out of existence.

Eventually, I sank down onto the ground, the snow

cushioning my knees. I scanned the forest, but it was futile. Zane was gone.

He'd left me.

He'd told me he loved me, and then he'd left me.

My heart shattered, and it hurt to breathe.

Someone came up from behind me and placed their hands on my shoulders. Nicole. She moved to stand in front of me and held out a hand to help me up.

I didn't take it. I just sat there, frozen in place, staring out at the path where Zane had disappeared.

"Summer," Nicole said, her voice muffled by the wind. "He's gone. We have to go back."

I forced my gaze away from the path to look up at her. "Why did he leave?" I croaked, as if she had a way of knowing.

"I don't know." Her voice was calm and understanding. "He said he trusted us. My best guess was that he was lying."

I scoffed at that. "Zane's good at lying."

Nicole's eyes narrowed. "Why do you say that?"

"Because he's been at the academy for two years, lying about his identity."

"True," she said, and she lowered herself so her eyes were level with mine. "Are you okay?"

"I don't know. He promised me he was on my side. And then…" I glanced over her shoulder at the path into the forest, the meaning clear.

And then he left me.

"You have no idea what was going on in his head," she said.

"He told me he loved me." I had trouble believing he'd said those words to me, but I did know this—Zane might be a good liar, but he wasn't lying about loving me.

At least, I hoped he wasn't.

Maybe I needed to stop being so naive. Maybe this was all one giant scheme of his, and he was using my emotions to his advantage. He was manipulative, he was cruel, and there was no reason for me to trust a thing he said.

Except...

"He said the hammer only creates electricity for a god," I said. "But it created electricity for me."

Nicole studied me, like she was searching for something she wasn't seeing. "I don't know much about the hammer," she said. "But Kate will. We have to get back and talk to her. She'll help us make sense of everything that just happened here."

"But Zane..." I looked around fruitlessly. I felt numb—like the icy air had frozen me in place.

"Zane left," Nicole said softly. "But he made sure we got back to the car. He wants us to get back to the academy safely."

"You don't know that."

"Maybe not. But sitting out here in the cold isn't going

to do anyone any good." She stood again and held out her hand. "We have to go."

The wind stopped, and I glanced around the forest again.

There was nothing.

Zane was gone. He wasn't coming back. Maybe not ever.

But he wouldn't do that. He wouldn't just *leave* me like that, with no explanation why.

Except he just did.

The truth was that I didn't know Zane very well at all. And I wasn't going to sit here in the forest, freezing to death and pining for him.

So I took Nicole's hand, stood up, and walked with her back to the car, where Blake was waiting patiently in the driver's seat.

He glanced over his shoulder at me as I got settled in the back. "You okay?" he asked.

"I don't know."

"Got it." He pulled the car out of the turn-off, and we started the long drive back to the academy.

I stared out the window, numb, replaying those final moments with Zane. I kept seeing that intense expression in his eyes when he said he loved me.

He'd meant it. I knew he did.

I should have said something—anything—back. Instead, I'd sat there like a mute idiot.

And then there was the part about the hammer.

I rested my head against the window. I was tired. My body was tired, my heart was tired—every piece of my soul was tired.

So I closed my eyes and drifted off to sleep, knowing that once we got back to the academy, all hell was going to break loose when we talked to Kate and analyzed everything that had happened these past few days in the Immortal Mountains.

CHAPTER FORTY-ONE

Nicole woke me up when we got back to the academy, and the three of us walked to the cottage in silence.

Now that we were back, the entire experience in the mountains felt like a strange dream.

The biggest reminder that it had all actually happened was that Zane and Mason weren't here with us. Although, Mason had technically never been with us. He'd been Loki the entire time.

It was a Thursday night, so the campus was pretty busy with students coming and going from their dorms to the dining hall. They watched us when we walked by, although none of them said anything.

Where did they think we'd been these past few days? How much had Kate told them about what we'd been doing? Probably not much, given that the student body knew nothing about the Norse gods and the threat they were bringing to us.

We got to the cottage, and Blake opened the door so Nicole and I could enter first.

Kate waited for us in the living room, with one of the many books from the coffee table open on her lap. In the car, Nicole had texted her the basics of what was going on, so she could start researching.

"Good. You're here." Kate placed the book down, the pages open to keep her place. "Nicole told me a bit about what happened, but I think it's best that I hear the whole story from you."

"Right," I said, and we all sat down and filled Kate in on everything from the beginning.

She was calm and poised, listening without saying much of anything. It was eerie—I had no idea what was going through her mind.

The entire time, I was scared she was going to blame me for what had happened.

I wouldn't blame her if she did. I deserved it. Deep down, I'd always known the secrets were going to catch up to me.

The biggest question was what type of punishment I'd have to pay.

We reached the end, and Nicole had to tell Kate the part about Zane leaving. I couldn't bring myself to say it out loud.

"We have a lot to unpack here," Kate said once we'd finished.

"Yeah," I said, and then I felt a familiar itching at the back of my neck. I turned around, chills running up my spine as I caught my own reflection in a small handheld mirror that was opened like a clam. The surface of it glimmered, as if something was moving inside of it.

Kate stood and walked toward it. "I could have sworn I'd closed that," she said, but I hurried past her, taking the mirror in my hand before she could reach it.

I held it close to my face and stared intently into my eyes, trying to see into the other side. There was nothing other than my reflection, but from the chills on my neck, I knew someone was looking back at me.

"I know you're there." I tried to sound as confident and menacing as I could. "Show yourself."

Nothing happened. Not even a shimmer.

"Who are you?" I shouted into the mirror this time, as if they'd hear me better that way.

Nothing.

Anger coursed through me—about all the secrets I'd had to keep, about Zane's mood swings and his leaving me, about being stupid enough to hand the hammer over to Mason/Loki—and I screamed, throwing the mirror as hard as I could.

It banged against the wall and shattered to the ground.

I breathed heavily as I stared down at it.

That hadn't felt nearly as good as I'd wanted it to.

"Oh my God." Nicole's lips parted into a giant O, as if she'd just had a major revelation.

"What?" I asked.

"This is going to sound crazy," she said, and I watched her, waiting for her to continue. "But I think the person watching us is Persephone."

CHAPTER FORTY-TWO

"What?" I stared at Nicole, dumbfounded.

"Persephone is Hades' wife," she said quickly.

"I know that," I said slowly, since didn't everyone know that? "But why do you think she's watching us?"

"Because she has a magic mirror." She ran her fingers through her hair, frustrated with herself. "I can't believe I didn't remember it sooner. She told us about the mirror when Blake and I visited the Underworld a few years ago. It was a gift from Hades. He knew how much she missed her family when she was in the Underworld, so he gave her a mirror she could look into and watch what was happening on Earth. She can't communicate through it, but it allows her to check in on her loved ones and see how they're doing. She told us it makes her time in the Underworld more bearable."

I kept staring at the shattered mirror, taking it all in. "I thought it was the Norse gods spying on us," I said simply. "Or the immortals."

"The immortals wouldn't have needed to spy on us through mirrors." Blake scowled. "They had Zane and Vera for that."

I flinched at Zane's name. And at the fact that Blake was likely right.

"It makes so much sense." Nicole jumped in excitement. "Especially because it's winter, which is when Persephone spends her time in the Underworld."

I switched my focus to Kate, since she knew more than all of us combined.

"It's a good theory," she said. "Especially because Summer's the only one who's mentioned feeling like someone's watching her through the mirrors."

"You think Persephone wants to spy on me because her husband is my father?" I asked, since it made sense when put that way.

"No," she said. "I think Persephone's watching you because she wants to check in on her daughter."

I stared at her, taking a few seconds to digest what she was saying. "Wait," I finally said. "Do you mean *me?*"

"Wow." Nicole looked at me with awe in her eyes. "No way. I mean, I guess it makes sense. But..." She trailed off, as if she couldn't find the right words.

Kate stood, picked up one of the many potted plants

on the windowsill, and placed it down on the coffee table next to the open book. There were no flowers on it, but its buds showed it wouldn't be long until there were. "I want you to make the flowers bloom," she said.

"You really think Persephone is my birth mother?" I ignored the plant, my mind stuck on what she'd just said.

"I think there's a chance," she said. "It's the best lead we have about the identity of your bio-mom."

"But Persephone and Hades are gods," I said. "And when two gods have a child..." I trailed off, since the obvious conclusion was totally absurd.

"Then that child is a god," Kate finished. "Which would explain why Thor's Hammer ignited when you held it."

"You're saying I'm a goddess."

"I don't think it's impossible."

"But wouldn't you have been able to tell? Wouldn't I have some sort of goddess glow or something?"

"You do have a 'goddess glow,'" Nicole chimed in. "You're super intimidating. Of course, *I'm* not intimidated, but pretty much everyone else is. We assumed it's because you're a daughter of Hades. But being a goddess actually makes a ton of sense."

Kate motioned toward the plant. "Give it a go."

"Sure," I said, since I had nothing to lose. And when I reached out with my mind, the energy of the plant answered me. It was like when I reached out for metal and gems.

Come to life, I thought, doing my best to speak in my mind to the flowers.

Nothing happened.

So I reached out more, wrapping my magic around the buds like tentacles.

Open for me, I urged.

The skin of the buds peeled away, and the bright pink flowers inside shimmered as they bloomed to life.

I stared at them in awe.

"It's official." Kate smiled. "You have earth magic."

I sat down, stunned, even though my earth magic wasn't surprising after the way I'd fought Topher on the field and what I'd done in the cave. "But I don't understand," I said. "If Persephone knows I'm her daughter, why didn't she say something? She's only in the Underworld during the winter. In the summer, she's here. She could have found me. She could have been in my life."

"I don't have an answer for you," Kate said. "But I can think of a person who does."

"My mom." The answer came to me instantly.

"Yes."

"But she's been MIA since the last time we spoke here. She hasn't picked up when I've called. She hasn't even answered my texts." I pulled out my phone, pressed her name, and put it on speaker to prove it.

The call rang through without her picking up.

"You need to be more aggressive than that," Blake said. "Text her. Tell her what we know."

"Okay." I typed out the text, then pressed send. The words didn't feel real as I wrote them out.

I know Persephone's my birth mother. Come to the cottage. I need answers.

My heart pounded as I stared at the blue text bubble.

Fifteen minutes. Her answer came quickly, and I relayed it to the others.

Kate asked if we wanted anything to drink, and she returned with what we'd requested. After days of living off melted snow and ice, the familiar taste of Coke was positively delicious.

Fifteen minutes later, my mom entered the cottage from a swirling dark fog near the front door. She wore jeans and a flowing purple shirt, and from the way her long dark hair blew around her, it was obvious that she was an otherworldly goddess.

"How did you do that?" I asked.

"I can travel through the shadows of the Underworld," she said simply, as if it was as normal as flying here in a plane.

"Got it," I said.

"So." She took a deep breath and rubbed her hands over her jeans. "You figured it out."

"You mean we're right?" I asked, shocked.

"Yes," she said. "You are."

CHAPTER FORTY-THREE

"But *how*?" I asked. "You said that Hades couldn't know I existed. Wouldn't he have known if his wife was pregnant and gave birth?"

"Persephone spends half her time in the Underworld, and the other half on Earth," my mom said. "She realized she was pregnant near the end of her stay in the Underworld. She wasn't showing, so she was able to hide it. Then, when she returned to Earth for the spring and summer, she went through the remainder of her pregnancy and gave birth to you. Her beautiful summer child."

"That's how she chose my name," I realized.

"Correct." Her eyes twinkled as she smiled at me.

"And then she gave me to you to raise?"

"Correct again," she said. "As I said before, I'm able to travel in the shadows of the Underworld. When your mother comes and goes each season, I'm the one who escorts her. We've become the best of friends. I helped her through her pregnancy, and it was her greatest wish that you lived on Earth and not have to endure life in the Underworld as she does. She wanted your life to be full and carefree for as long as possible. When she asked, I was more than happy to raise you and protect you."

"And she watches me," I said. "Through the mirrors."

"She does."

"But she comes to Earth each summer," I said. "How come she never visits me?"

"I don't know," my mom answered truthfully. "I've always suspected it would be too hard on her. Your mother is kind and loving—it's what drew Hades to her. And it's truly her greatest wish for you to never have to live in the Underworld. I think she did everything she could to make that happen—even though it meant she could never be an actual part of your life."

I frowned, surprised by the tears threatening to leak out of my eyes.

"But she loves you with all her heart," my mom said quickly. "I'm sure of it."

I sipped my Coke, needing something to do as I took all this in. It was a lot. Especially after everything that had happened over the past few weeks. My brain was spinning out of control, but I did my best to focus and calm it down.

One thing at a time. I could handle it. I'd kept myself together this far. I could keep going.

Giving up wasn't an option. I *had* to keep going.

"I want to meet her," I decided. "Can you make that happen?"

My mom nodded, as if she'd expected as much. "It's winter right now, so she's in the Underworld," she said. "I fetch her in spring, when the flowers are ready to bloom. Once she's safely back on Earth, I'll talk to her."

"Thank you," I said. "I appreciate it."

"After everything, it's the least I can do."

"This is all very interesting," Blake broke into the conversation. "And definitely something to discuss further—later. Because we have other problems to address right now. Mainly, the fact that the Norse gods are trying to release Odin and the Valkyries, and that once they do, they're going to launch a war on us. We have to focus on stopping them."

"We do," Kate agreed. "But something about what you've told me isn't adding up."

"What's that?" he asked.

"How does Zane have all of this information about Odin and the Valkyries?"

She looked to me, and I shrugged.

"I don't know," I said. "He had a lot of secrets. I know there was a lot he was keeping from me."

"Clearly." Blake scoffed.

THE SECRETS OF MAGIC   317

I narrowed my eyes at him.

"I think the immortals have more to do with this than he told us," Kate continued, and I said nothing, since she was right.

"Why?" I asked.

"From what I've been reading, the immortals like to stay out of conflict. But they still cause it. And I know Zane claimed the immortals aren't taking sides in all of this, but I don't believe him. Especially given the way he ran off."

"Agreed," Nicole said. "But he's gone now. It's not like we can question him."

Question him.

My mind flashed to the memory of Fulla locked in her torture cell, and relief filled me at the knowledge that Zane had avoided a fate like that.

"We might not be able to question him," Kate said, focusing on me. "But you can."

"What do you mean?" I asked. "Zane might be my soulmate, but we don't have a telepathic bond. He's as gone to me as he is to you."

"But he said he'll always protect you," she said. "And he loves you."

"Yeah." My heart leaped at the memory of his confession.

"He meant it," Nicole chimed in. "I could tell."

"But what do you want me to *do* about it?" I asked.

"Go back to the mountains and find him so I can force the answers out of him myself?"

The others were quiet. Even my mom.

"Wait," I said. "That's not really what you want me to do. Is it?"

"It's actually a pretty good idea," Blake mused.

I turned to Nicole, hoping she'd be a voice of reason. Which I instantly knew was silly, since Nicole was a "jump into the action and take risks" sort of person.

"It's a *great* idea," she said, and I couldn't help it—I rolled my eyes.

I looked back to my mom, curious about her thoughts. There was no way she'd be okay with this crazy plan.

"As you know, Persephone can watch out for you in the mirrors," she said calmly. "Carry one with you at all times. If it gets too dangerous up there and you need help, ask Persephone through the mirrors. She'll get the message to me, and I can come to you through the shadows."

"The immortals won't take kindly to you being there," Kate said. "They don't like the Norse gods, but they hate us even more. You'd be risking yourself."

"I'd be risking myself *for my daughter*," she said. "It's a risk worth taking."

"You're agreeing to this," I said flatly, unable to believe it.

"Zane loves you," she said softly. "You're his soulmate. If anyone can find out what the immortals are up to, it's you."

"And you need to do anything you can to get them to trust you," Kate added. "Even if it means hurting us in the process."

"You want me to spy on them," I realized. "Just like Zane and Vera spied on us."

"I do," she said. "And then, with the knowledge you obtain, we'll take down the Norse and the immortals, and stop this war before it has a chance to begin."

I wanted to tell them that I knew more than I'd said earlier. But what did I *truly* know? Zane had lied so much. There was no way to know which parts were true, and which were lies. And there was probably so much more beneath the surface that I wasn't privy to. Information that could help us face the Norse gods *and* the immortals when the time came.

If I claimed my soulmate bond with Zane and pretended to join the immortals, they'd include me in their plans as if I was one of them.

Maybe.

Hopefully.

"You're our secret weapon," Blake repeated what he'd told me all those days ago. "You can help us win this war from the inside. So, tell us—are you in, or out?"

I looked around at their eager faces, knowing exactly what I had to do. Because these people were my family.

I'd do anything to help them. The thought of walking straight into enemy territory was terrifying, but Zane had made it clear to me that I wasn't his enemy, and that his people wouldn't consider me one, either.

"I'm in," I said, the words feeling *right* after I spoke them.

"Good." Nicole nodded in approval. "Then let's get focused and start strategizing. Because it's time for the real games to begin."

FROM THE AUTHOR

I hope you enjoyed *The Secrets of Magic!* If so, I'd love if you left a review. Reviews help readers find the book, and I read each and every one of them. They also motivate me to write the next book faster!

A review for the first book in the series is the most helpful.

To chat with me and other readers about the book, go to www.facebook.com/groups/michellemadow and join my Facebook group.

The next book in the Elementals Academy series, *The Queen of Magic,* is releasing in winter 2022.

Pre-order your copy now at:
mybook.to/elementalsacademy3

Sign up to my email list to get an email when the book releases:
michellemadow.com/subscribe

If you haven't read the original Elementals series yet, I recommend checking it out while you wait for the next Elementals Academy book. It starts with *The Prophecy of Shadows*, and is about Nicole and the original Elementals. You can grab it on Amazon now.

I hope you enjoy Elementals: The Prophecy of Shadows!

CONNECT WITH MICHELLE

Never miss a new release by signing up to get emails or texts when Michelle's books come out.

Sign up for emails: michellemadow.com/subscribe
Sign up for texts: michellemadow.com/texts

Social Media Links:

Facebook Group: facebook.com/groups/michellemadow
Instagram: @michellemadow
Email: michelle@madow.com
Website: www.michellemadow.com

ABOUT THE AUTHOR

Michelle Madow is a *USA Today* bestselling author of fast-paced fantasy novels that will leave you turning the pages wanting more! Her books are full of magic, adventure, romance, and twists you'll never see coming.

Michelle grew up in Maryland, and now lives in Florida. She's loved reading for as long as she can remember. She wrote her first book in her junior year of college and hasn't stopped writing since! She also loves traveling, and has been to all seven continents. Someday, she hopes to travel the world for a year on a cruise ship.

Never miss a new release by signing up to get emails or texts when Michelle's books come out:

Sign up for emails: michellemadow.com/subscribe
Sign up for texts: michellemadow.com/texts

Connect with Michelle:

Facebook Group: facebook.com/groups/michellemadow
Instagram: @michellemadow
Email: michelle@madow.com
Website: www.michellemadow.com

Printed in Great Britain
by Amazon